INSTITUTE OF MAGIC

DRAGON'S GIFT THE DRUID BOOK 1

LINSEY HALL

For Lindsay and Andrew.

1

The Edinburgh alley stank of dark magic and pee. Which made it perfect for one of the Academy's obstacle courses. The Undercover Protectorate really liked to chuck its trainees into the deep end, after all.

For a magical mess like me, this was *whoa* deep.

I crouched lower in the alley as I waited for the race to start and searched the darkened street ahead. Rain pattered on the cobblestones that gleamed beneath the streetlamp. My competitors were hiding in other alleys, but we'd all begin as soon as the clock tolled midnight.

"How's it going, Ana?" Bree's voice whispered out of the comms charm around my neck.

"Oh, fab." I grinned. "About to run into a death trap. My favorite way to spend a Friday night."

"It's the only way we spend Friday nights."

"True." If I wasn't training to join the Protectorate, I was helping my sister Bree with one of her assignments. They were always deadly, of course. She'd finished the Academy in record time and had graduated to taking on investigative cases.

I, on the other hand, was taking my own sweet time.

Some might call me overly cautious. I called it smart.

The reality was that I had almost no magic. Which you kind of needed to get through a magical academy that fed into a prestigious institute dedicated to helping supernaturals in need.

I squinted into the street ahead, but nothing moved. No clues about what was to come but also no cars. Then the clock chimed midnight, the bells tolling through the city. My heart jumped.

"Gotta go, Bree," I said. "Time to run."

Literally. Whatever the Protectorate might throw at me on this course, I knew I'd be running for my life.

"I'll be here," Bree said.

I grinned and touched my fingertips to the charm, glad to have my sister at my side. Bree was a Valkyrie, with wings and everything. She hovered high above, keeping track of the contestants' progress. She couldn't help me, but she could update me a bit.

My heart thundered as I sprinted into the street. It was dead silent. I glanced left and right, spotting the three other trainees as they darted out from their alleys. We'd all take different routes through the city as we raced to capture the flags at the other side.

Last one loses; incompetent ones might die.

A deadly supernatural game of capture the flag.

As I raced across the street, a rumbling underfoot made my skin chill. A second later, the cobblestones dropped away as the ground beneath me disappeared. I leapt and barely landed on solid ground, then sprinted ahead. All around me, portions of the street dropped away.

A scream sounded from one of my competitors, but I didn't look. I couldn't. Not if I wanted to keep my eye on the ground and save myself from falling into the earth.

Yep. That was goal number one.

I might not have enough magic, but I had a lot of practice trying to stay alive.

I jumped from cobblestone to cobblestone as the street fell away around me. Sweat dripped down my back as I ran. Man, a bit of levitation magic would come in handy right now.

At the Academy, the more magic you had, the easier it was to pass. Not good news for me. My only magic was the ability to create an invisible shield to protect me from threats.

I made the last jump to the other side of the street and kept running, sprinting toward another alley. Like my competitors, I'd memorized the map of the city and had already chosen my route—I just had to hope there weren't too many obstacles.

The Undercover Protectorate was an institute dedicated to helping supernaturals with problems that were so dangerous the magical government didn't want to handle them. A lot of those folks lived here, in the Grassmarket, the supernatural district of Edinburgh. This area was hidden from humans by a spell called the Great Peace, and it was a haven for our kind.

In return for our help, the residents of the Grassmarket kindly loaned out their neighborhood for the Protectorate Academy's training runs. They even helped with the obstacles.

Lucky me.

I ducked down an alley to the left. It was dark and narrow. Glowing green eyes peered out at me from a hole in the wall. I sprinted by, panting.

Please don't jump on me, creature.

The little beast hissed, but didn't lash out.

A cat?

I didn't take the time to look closely.

"How's it going?" Bree asked from my comms charm.

"Fab. Most fun ever." I panted, darting right, down a wider

street. Shops and restaurants lined both sides, but they were closed at this hour.

Light glowed from one up ahead. *Shit.*

I crossed to the opposite side of the street and raced down the sidewalk, hoping I was making good time. A shadow filled the lighted doorway of the shop up ahead.

Ah, crap.

The figure hurled something at me. A small flash of blue caught my eye.

Potion bomb!

Shit, who knew what was in that?

I flung out my arm, calling upon my magic to create a shield. It swelled inside me, bursting forth to create a barrier of white light.

The potion bomb smashed into the shield, shattering. The scent of dirty socks filled the air, a clear sign of magic meant to harm. Dark magic always smelled bad—just depended on what kind of bad.

I sprinted faster, nearing the figure in the door. It was an older woman, a grin stretching across her face. She threw another potion bomb—a green one this time.

Acid, if I had to bet.

I kept my shield in place, and the bomb smashed against it, reeking like week-old tuna fish. I gagged and scowled at her.

It was all I could do, since she was one of the residents who'd agreed to help with the course. I couldn't exactly nail her with one of my favorite daggers.

Bad form and all that.

"How am I doing on time?" I asked Bree.

"Pretty good. Lavender looks like she's in the lead, though."

Damn.

I sprinted past the woman, who hurled one last potion

bomb. It shattered against my shield, the scent of decaying flowers filling my nose.

A block later, I stumbled out into a courtyard. Six demons lingered there, lounging on benches around a fountain. Large oak trees dotted the space, their autumn leaves orange and bright. Moonlight gleamed on the demons' large horns and the weapons hanging from their clothing.

Crap.

The real challenge.

Demons were the Protectorate's most common magical foe. There were hundreds of species, all originating from the different underworlds, and they usually worked as mercenaries. Occasionally, the Protectorate hired them as part of the obstacle courses.

Bad news for me.

These guys would shoot to kill, no holds barred.

No one ever said making it through the Academy was easy.

A small demon with gleaming red eyes caught sight of me. He stood on spindly legs, pointing a long claw at me. "She's here!"

His voice sounded like it filtered through gravel in his throat.

I drew a dagger from the ether, the magical substance that filled the air, invisible and soundless. They were my weapons of choice, and the magic that allowed me to store them in the ether had been expensive.

Worth it, though, for someone like me. When all you had was defensive magic in an offensive world, you had to get good with steel.

I hurled the dagger. It glinted in the moonlight as it spun end over end and then sank into a big green demon's neck. Blood spurted and he fell, crashing onto his back.

His compatriots roared.

The little demon flung out his hands, sending a bolt of lightning toward me. Thunder cracked as the light nearly blinded me. I lunged behind a dumpster, skidding on some slimy stuff that reeked of garbage, then scrambled to my feet, peering around the edge of the dumpster.

The demons were advancing on me, five different species with five different types of magic. The red one looked like a fire demon, and the gray a smoke demon.

Damn.

My heart thundered. I was *way* outnumbered.

When the red demon hurled a massive fireball at the dumpster, my stomach dropped. It collided with the huge metal canister just as I lunged out from my hiding space. The dumpster flew backward against the wall, crashing into the bricks.

The trash ignited as I sprinted along the side of the courtyard, drawing a dagger from the ether.

I threw it, aiming for the fire demon's neck. He dodged, and my blade sank into his chest. He stumbled, going to his knees.

Damn it!

Not a kill shot. It was always so hard to tell with demons where their heart would be.

I drew another dagger as I sprinted for cover. My magical shield worked both ways—nothing could come in, but nothing could go out, either. Meaning no weapons.

If my options were cowering behind my magic or running and fighting, I'd take the latter any day.

I pulled a dagger from the ether, aiming it at the smoke demon. Before I had a chance to throw, a blast of gray smoke shot from his hands, hurtling toward me. I dived out of the way, but not before a third demon threw a huge icicle.

The frozen spear shot through the air and sliced across my thigh like a blade. Pain flared as I crashed to the ground. The ball of smoke hit a tree behind me, blasting away the leaves and many of the branches.

I scrambled upright and drew a dagger from the ether, calling on the muscle memory of thousands of hours of practice. I hurled it, taking out the smoke demon with a precise blow to the neck. It was really the only way to go—chests were too iffy and skulls were too hard.

He gurgled, blood spurting, as he fell to his knees.

The remaining three demons roared. The little lightning demon's hands crackled with light around the claws—he was charged up and ready to hurl another bolt. A creepy white demon unhinged his jaw, opening it wide to reveal six-inch fangs.

Please, don't be super fast.

I didn't want him sinking those chompers into me.

The ice demon's skin glowed blue and pale, looking cold even from this distance, and the wounded fire demon was staggering to his feet. Flames blazed around his hands, and vengeance burned in his eyes.

Oh boy. I was in big freaking trouble and way outnumbered.

I sprinted for cover behind another dumpster as I hurled my dagger at him, aiming for the neck. It sank into his flesh, sending him flying backward.

Points for me!

Except then the white demon with the long fangs split himself in two and became two separate demons. Then three.

Oh crap.

"Hurry up, Ana!" Bree said. "Lavender is getting close to the finish line. Angus isn't far behind."

Shit. I was losing *and* I was about to be killed by demons. The lightning demon raised his hands and shot a bolt at me. I called on my magic, throwing out my shield just in time. The lightning plowed into the shield, making the barrier flare white as it took the damage. My arms shook with the force of it, and sweat popped out on my brow. I squinted, trying to see through my whitened shield.

What the hell?

It looked like tiny figures were flying through the air.

I dropped my shield, darting right as I pulled a dagger from the ether. My vision narrowed in on a small creature leaping from the top of a tree onto the lightning demon. It landed on the demon's chest and tore out its throat.

The little monster was hairless with a long tail and big ears.

A hairless cat?

I hurled my dagger at the blue ice demon. It hit the mark and blood sprayed, but not before he fired one last icicle at me. I dived out of the way, my wounded leg singing with pain.

As I crashed to the ground, I caught sight of a fluffy white ball of fur leaping out of a tall tree. It landed on one of the white demons, sending him crashing back into the fountain. Blood sprayed as the white fluff-ball tore out the demon's throat.

Holy crap, that was a cat!

There were now only two of the white fangy demons left. One of them raced for me, unnaturally fast. I drew a dagger and nailed him in the throat just as a third cat streaked across the cobblestone courtyard and leapt onto the last demon.

The tiny orange cat mauled the monster, fangs and claws flying. A creature that small shouldn't be able to cause so much damage!

The white Persian was streaked with blood, and the black hairless cat looked like it was having a grand time surveying the carnage all around.

Eight demon bodies were disappearing back to their underworlds, where they'd wake up eventually and try to get back to earth.

"Ana! You gotta get going!" Bree's voice rang through the comms charm.

I gave the cats one last look. "Thanks, guys."

They stared at me silently, and I sprinted away, determined to make up for lost time. I didn't know who my feline helpers were, but I didn't have time to find out.

No way I wanted to be last in a challenge *again.*

Eventually the Protectorate might just kick me out.

I didn't stop to retrieve my weapons. The expensive spell that stored them in the ether would do that for me. It wouldn't clean them, unfortunately, so I'd have to take care of the demon blood myself, but I'd deal with that later.

"I'm going through the graveyard," I said.

"No!" Bree shouted. "Too dangerous."

She was right. And sure, it wasn't part of my original route since the shortcut went through one of the most deadly parts of Edinburgh, but I wasn't willing to come in last. Normally I was a Plan B and C kinda girl—and this was Plan B.

Risky, but worth it.

I raced toward the wrought iron fence that surrounded the ancient burial site. The gate was locked so I went to the left and scrambled up and over the iron fence.

As soon as I hit the ground on the other side, a chill of fear raced over me. Mist hovered just above the ground, twining around the headstones that glowed pale gray in the moonlight. It was unnaturally cold here, even for Scotland in the fall.

I sucked in a ragged breath and ran, cutting through the headstones and praying that no ghosts waited for me.

When the temperature dropped to an unnatural chill, my heart thundered wildly.

Oh no.

The silvery blue glow rising up from the ground filled me with fear, acidic and sharp.

Phantoms.

The silvery blue light coalesced to form figures—all of them dressed in old-style clothes, the styles of which spanned thousands of years. Fancy ladies with tall hair and knights in armor. Cave men wearing furs and monks draped in cowls. Their eyes were black pits that zeroed in on me as they raised their hands and drifted nearer.

Phantoms were far worse than ghosts.

I called upon my shield, praying it would work for this. The magic flared within me, shooting out to form a protective dome over me as I ran.

But the crowd of Phantoms was too big. Their hunger too great. They collided with my shield, unable to pass through. Their magic leached through the barrier, however, reaching inside my mind and going for my worst memories.

"Protect your mind!" Bree cried through the comms charm. "Don't let them in!"

Tears filled my eyes as I fought their magic and failed. The icy tendrils of their magic slipped inside my head, weaseling into my brain. I stumbled, stomach lurching.

"Failure," one hissed.

"Magical nothing," whispered another.

"Dead weight," said a third.

They were finding my worst fears. They pushed harder inside my head, sending an icepick of pain through my mind. Phantoms didn't speak like people—they reflected your fears back at you, using your mind.

And fates, it *sucked*.

"Think happy thoughts!" Bree cried.

Ha ha. Right.

All I could see was myself, failing and being thrown out of the Protectorate, having to leave Bree and Rowan, my sisters. Being forced into the outside world where my kind was hunted because we were capable of too much magic. A life on the streets, alone.

I was a Dragon God whose magic hadn't developed yet. Supposedly, I would inherit the magic of dragons and gods—but I hadn't. Not like my sister had, at least. Which left me vulnerable.

The Phantoms grabbed onto that, magnifying the fear.

"It never will," hissed a phantom wearing the robe of a monk. "Powerless forever."

"Worthless," whispered one to my left.

I sobbed and pushed myself harder, running past the monsters. Sweat dampened my skin. I had to make it past the Phantoms!

I couldn't let these miserable, dead jerks take me down.

I focused on the thought, on the will to survive. To win.

I wouldn't be beaten.

I wouldn't give up.

If they stopped me, they would win. My worst fears would come true.

I'd lose my new home. Lose my sisters. Lose everything.

My lungs burned as I ran, dodging headstones and the magical grip of the Phantoms. But their magic slowed me, making my legs feel like they weighed a thousand pounds.

A blur of movement near the ground caught my eye.

Three little figures, racing alongside me.

The cats?

They hissed at the Phantoms, deep sounds of venomous rage that made my skin chill.

The Phantoms fell back, just slightly. It was enough that I could pick up speed and push past them.

The iron fence appeared through the mist.

Almost there!

I sprinted for it, leaping over it so fast I stumbled on the other side. The cats slipped through the fence bars, following me as I ran down a street.

I was almost there. Sweat chilled my skin and my lungs burned as I ran. I shot out into the courtyard that marked the finish line. Just in time to see another competitor race toward the last remaining flag and grab it off the post.

My heart dropped.

The three other members of my class already stood within the circle, each gripping a flag in their hand.

There were no more flags left.

I was last.

Shit.

I slowed to a walk, determined not to show my disappointment. Maybe I'd gotten unlucky and my route was harder? Or maybe I sucked at this.

But moping wouldn't change anything. A stiff upper lip would do wonders, though. The ol' pick-yourself-up-and-brush-yourself-off was my familiar friend.

"Sorry, man," Bree murmured from my comms charm.

I looked up, catching sight of her hovering high in the sky. Her silver wings gleamed in the moonlight.

I smiled up at her, then approached the group. My three classmates were all in their late teens and early twenties like me. Jude, the head of the Undercover Protectorate, was a striking woman in her mid-thirties. Her dark skin gleamed in the light of the moon and her blue eyes sparkled with stars in their depths. Long braids stretched down her back.

Jude ran the Paranormal Investigative Team, the unit that Bree had joined when she'd graduated from the Academy. Our other friends were part of that unit as well. It was the most prestigious, and Jude always oversaw the obstacle course. Since I wanted to join my sister in her unit—the PITs as they were laughingly called—I'd usually be glad to talk to Jude.

Now that I'd come in last?

Yeah, not my best moment. Skulking around in the shadows sounded good right about now.

I stiffened my spine and stopped in front of everyone, keeping my eyes off the red flags gripped in their hands. Lavender shot me a victorious look, and I wanted to kick her.

So I wasn't a good loser. Sue me.

"Well done, everyone," Jude said, but I swore her eyes gleamed with disappointment when she looked at me. Confusion, at least, since I was supposed to be an all-powerful Dragon God like my sister, but I was decidedly *not*. "You all did—" Her voice trailed off as her gaze drifted behind me, spotting something.

I turned, seeing the three cats who'd helped me along the way. They sat about fifteen feet behind me. This close, the hairless black one—a sphynx—looked like a beat-up old tom who'd seen a lot in his day. A white spot marked his chest, his whiskers were frazzled, and his green eyes blazed at me. A matching emerald earring pierced his left ear. Magic filled the air around him, an unusual signature of green grass.

"Meow." *You are gazing upon the great Muffin of the Highlands!*

I shook my head. Was I hearing him in my head?

Of course you are, you ninny. Do you think magical cats just meow?

A magical cat.

"But...Muffin?" I asked.

What? Muffin is a fine name! He looked toward the white cat and muttered, *I really thought she'd be more impressed.*

"I am!"

He shot me a look that said he didn't buy it, then nodded at the white cat. *That is Princess Snowflake III.*

Next to him, the fluffy white Persian licked blood from her chops. Her fangs were unusually long—perfect for tearing the throats out of demons. The fat diamond hanging around her neck was splattered with blood. She glared at me with an evil eye, belying her pretty face and fur.

At her side, the small orange cat licked his butt. He looked up, fur disheveled on top of his head and sporting a goofy grin. He wore no jewels, but then, he didn't seem like the type.

Muffin meowed. *And that is Bojangles.*

For fate's sake—Bojangles?

Who the heck were these three?

"Did you pick up some friends?" Jude asked.

I looked away from the cats and met her gaze. "I'm not sure. But I think they must be a local cat gang," I joked, hiking a thumb at the black sphynx, Muffin. "He's the leader."

Muffin gave a deep meow, as if he agreed with me.

"Actually, those are the Cats of Catastrophe," Angus said, his Edinburgh accent thick. He was the only local member of my class. "They *are* a local cat gang. They run a racket down by the docks, tricking the fishermen into giving them fish."

"And stealing," Jude said. "I've never seen the Cats of Catastrophe before, but I've heard of them. They run jewel heists on the Royal Mile."

"*Jewels?*" That explained how they'd gotten the sparkles, but still....

Actual cat burglars?

I turned back to look at the gang. Muffin had taken up with the butt licking, and the orange one was now bouncing around, chasing a bug. Princess Snowflake III continued to glare at me.

Why had they helped me?

As if she could read my thoughts, Jude said, "They chose you."

"I don't know why," I said. But I was grateful. I wouldn't have made it past the demons.

"Either way, it can only be a good thing," she said.

I hoped she was right, because I'd just totally biffed the

obstacle course and come in last. That was one more mark against me, setting me even farther back from graduating. Right now, I needed all the good things I could get. And if that was the assistance of a magical cat gang—which sounded ridiculous, frankly—I was going to take it.

2

As we all departed the clearing to head back to the Undercover Protectorate, Bree landed next to me, folding her silvery wings back into her body. Her dark hair shined in the moonlight, and sympathy gleamed in her eyes.

"Don't worry about me," I said, staving her off. "I'm fine. I'll get 'em next time."

"Jude said she'd never seen someone do so well against that many demons before." Bree tapped the golden comms charm around her neck. "She told me."

"I had my magical cat gang."

"*Without* them, she said. Though they did help with the end." She shook her head. "There were more demons than usual, according to Jude. Someone mistakenly hired too many. It wasn't fair."

I smiled at her. "Life isn't fair."

We'd been driven from our homes as children, hunted because we were Dragon Gods. Our mother had been killed by those who had stalked us—so I was very familiar with how *not fair* life was.

"Too true." Bree smiled and looped her arm through mine. "Come on. Let's go."

We followed the group back through the quiet streets of Edinburgh, hanging toward the back. Occasionally, I'd glance back to see if the cats were still following me.

They were.

Weird.

When we reached the main street in the Grassmarket, which had nothing at all to do with grass—at least not these days—we made our way quickly toward the portal that would take us to the Undercover Protectorate's castle. The portal sat within a darkened alley between a bar and a tartan shop, glowing blue and bright. Only members of the Protectorate could see and enter it.

I stepped through the portal last, letting the ether suck me in. It was a wild ride before it spat me out in a small enchanted forest in Northern Scotland. Night birds chirped, and the wind whistled through the ancient, twisted trees. The forest sat within the walls of the castle, and the portal connected it to the city, giving us easy access to everything we could want.

Bree stumbled out of the portal after me, grinning. "I love how close we are to downtown."

"Me too."

We hurried down the path that cut between the gnarled trees. Fairy lights danced around us, sparkling and bright, but the fae were long gone from here.

When we stepped out onto the rolling lawn that surrounded the castle, the moonlight gleamed on the massive structure that sat in the middle. Towers and turrets reached for the sky, while the mullioned glass glittered with golden light from within.

"I'll never get sick of it," Bree said.

"Same." The Protectorate had found us a few months ago

when we'd been in seriously dire straits, about to be killed by a wizard who we'd run afoul of.

Because of our rare magic, the Protectorate had invited us to work with them—if we could pass their training academy.

"At this rate, it's going to be years before I pass," I said.

"You're doing better than you think," Bree said.

I hoped she was right, because I really wanted to earn my place here.

The alternative was...unthinkable.

Ahead of us, Jude and the rest of the class hurried across the lawn to the castle, but Bree and I veered toward the old stables that sat near the huge wall that surrounded the castle grounds.

Rowan would be in there, no doubt, and we wanted to check up on her. A month ago, we'd rescued her from captivity. She'd spent five horrible years as a hostage, but she was starting to adjust well. Nothing kept Rowan down for long. There were still shadows in her eyes, but they were fading.

The old stone stables no longer contained horses, though the smell still lingered. Instead, it served as the castle's garage.

As expected, we found Rowan in the stables with the buggy, our souped-up monster truck that we'd brought with us from our old life. We'd joined the Protectorate back in the summer, leaving behind Death Valley Junction, a remote desert town full of supernaturals where we'd spent most of our lives hiding from the ones who hunted us.

We'd made a living by driving outlaws through Death Valley, and the buggy was the only thing that had helped us make it across safely. It was totally armored, covered with poisoned spikes, and outfitted with platforms from which to fight off the desert monsters who haunted the valley.

It'd been a fun life, but ultimately, we'd wanted more. And living out in the open had been too dangerous for Dragon Gods like ourselves. We were hunted and feared—folks either wanted to use us for our magic or kill us.

This was a safer life, and a better one. Here, we had an opportunity to do good in the world.

As long as I could pass the Academy.

In the stable, Rowan's booted feet stuck out from under the front of the buggy. It was my baby—I'd helped build every bit of it. If I could operate from this thing, I'd ace the Academy.

Unfortunately, that wasn't allowed.

Rowan rolled out from under the truck and grinned up at us. "How'd it go?"

"Not great." I winced at the memory of coming in last.

She stood, her black hair shining. She wore all black, too, looking stark and beautiful. "That's okay. You're still doing better than me."

Ever since her escape a month ago, she hadn't been able to access her magic. It could have been a result of trauma or something else, but we had no idea.

"You'll get it back."

"Maybe." She walked toward the side table and set down her wrench. "I'm working on it."

I needed to quit whining about my own problems. Rowan had it far worse than me, and she managed. True, she was up at three a.m. and working on the truck, so obviously she had some demons. But she wasn't a whiner.

Her gaze traveled past Bree and me, landing on the open door behind. "Who are they?"

I turned, spotting the Cats of Catastrophe. "My new friends, I think." I looked back at Rowan. "How's the engine? Making progress?"

"Yeah, it's tricky, but I'm almost there."

"I can help tomorrow." I wanted to. Working on the buggy

was one of my favorite things. It was soothing. Made me feel in control.

"We should all get some sleep," Bree said.

"Yeah." Rowan's jaw tightened.

"Nightmares?" I asked.

"Sometimes."

Always. It was unspoken but clear.

Footsteps sounded behind us, and I turned.

Caro appeared in the doorway, her short platinum bob gleaming. She was a water mage, and one of the members of the PITs, Jude's investigative team. She'd become our best friend here, along with Ali and Haris, who were behind her. The two dark-haired djinn's weren't kicking their usual hacky sack between them. That, combined with the worry on Caro's face, made nerves flutter in my stomach. She was usually smiling and peppy—albeit murderous with her water power—so this wasn't going to be good.

"Meeting time," Caro said. "We've got to hightail it to the round room."

"The round room?" Crap. That meant it was a big deal. I looked at the massive clock on the other side of the garage. Past 3 a.m., but if it was in the round room...

"Come on." Caro gestured for us to follow, and we did, flipping off the lights and shutting the door.

The round room was the equivalent of the Protectorate's war room. When something was really bad, all hands gathered in there. Most of the people were full-time staff who lived at and worked out of the castle, solving magical crimes and protecting those who couldn't protect themselves. There were only a few students at any given moment.

As the six of us walked across the lawn toward the castle, Caro chatted about castle gossip, with Ali and Haris chiming in occasionally. I glanced behind us. The cats were keeping up. As we stepped onto the stone-paved courtyard, the massive wooden doors swung open to permit us entrance.

I stepped through, glancing behind me one last time.

The Cats of Catastrophe strolled along behind us, eyes keen on me.

"Are you seriously following me *all the way* home?" I asked.

The sphinx gave a low, deep meow that sounded a heck of a lot like a yes. I turned back to enter the main hall, having no idea what to do about the cats.

"You've got sidekicks," Bree said.

A ghostly blue pug flew into the entry hall, transparent wings holding it aloft. The little creature had a big ham gripped in its teeth, but as soon as its gaze landed on Bree, it gave a yip of delight, managing not to drop the ham.

"Speaking of sidekicks." I pointed to Mayhem, who was most definitely Bree's sidekick.

Bree grinned at the little pug, who flew circles around her head. We headed toward the round room, with Mayhem leading the way down the stone corridor. The castle was huge, with many different construction styles from all periods in history. This hallway looked ancient, but others looked new—like a fancy mansion.

It was a long way from our old rundown place in Death Valley, that was for sure. We'd barely survived there, so this was a major upgrade.

I felt a prickle at the back of my neck, and I looked behind me.

The Cats of Catastrophe followed along, my silent shadows. I stopped and turned, putting my hands on my hips. "I really appreciate your help, guys. But I don't know if you're supposed to be here. I'm kinda new myself, so I can't really vouch for you."

Princess Snowflake III glared at me, the little orange one raced ahead to try to catch Mayhem, and Muffin licked his butt.

"You sure told them," Bree said.

I huffed a laugh. "As if I have any authority over cats."

I gave them one last look, then sighed and turned around.

As we approached the round room, a strange sense of power rolled out from it. Someone in there was *strong*.

Stronger than almost any of the supernaturals here, besides Bree—who'd fully come into her Dragon God power—and her boyfriend Cade, a Celtic war god.

I gasped. "Do you feel that?"

"Yeah." Rowan turned around to look at us, eyes wide. "Mega powerful."

"Must be part of the problem," Bree said. "Power like that always comes with problems."

"Isn't that the truth?" Our massive power—or at least, our potential for power, in my case—had kept us on the run for over a decade.

I slowed as I neared the entrance to the round room, drawing in the heady sense of magic that flowed out. There were dozens of magical signatures. Each type of supernatural had their own, and they generally correlated to one of the five senses. Or more than one sense, if you had a lot of magic.

But one person in there was *seriously* powerful and wasn't afraid to let it be known. While it was possible to hide your magical signature if you had the skill, this person clearly felt no need.

The room was crowded when we entered. The big round table had been removed, and the space was filled with people sitting in folding chairs. A crowd had gathered near the front, so I couldn't see who was standing up there, but I craned my neck to get a look at the person with the powerful magic. All I saw was a sea of heads and horns and wings—the Protectorate was full of all sorts.

We found a seat in the back, and the three Cats of Catastrophe joined us, each taking a seat for themselves.

"What the heck?" I muttered.

At the front, Jude clapped loudly and shouted, "Take your seats!"

People sat, and I got my first glimpse of the person with the power. My breath whooshed out of me.

Thank fates I was seated.

The man standing at the front was insanely beautiful—in a raw, powerful kind of way. He had to be well over six feet tall. Though he wore dark jeans and a black jacket, it wasn't hard to see that he was built like a boxer.

But his face...

Like a fallen angel, here to deliver justice. But a dark angel, with black hair and eyes. Handsome, yet a tiny bit scary in his perfection.

I swallowed hard.

Next to me, Rowan whistled low in her throat. "Who's the hottie?"

His eyes shifted toward us, passing over Rowan and landing on me.

Where they stayed.

Suddenly, it was hard to breathe. Not because he had some kind of power over me, but because I was some kind of infatuated moron. Which was a power in itself, actually.

And that annoyed the crap out of me.

I scowled at him, giving him my best hairy eyeball.

His brows rose.

With our gazes locked, it was impossible not to notice his magical signatures. Despite the dozens filling the room, his signatures cut through the others, rolling over me in waves.

His magic sounded like the low roll of distant thunder and

smelled like leather and pine. It tasted of caramel and surrounded him in an aura of silver light. But the feel of it...

Like a caress against my skin. Or a warm hug. Touching.

Lots and lots of touching.

Heat filled me.

"Quit it," I mouthed at him.

He just stared at me, a curious look in his dark eyes.

Jude stepped forward, her starry blue eyes sparkling in the light. The Undercover Protectorate was made up of different divisions—the Demon Trackers Unit, Interspecies Mediation, Research and Development, and the Paranormal Investigative Team—but if she was taking the lead, this must be some kind of issue that needed the investigative team.

"Lachlan Munroe has a job for us," she said. "The biggest one in recent history, which leads to this all-hands-on-deck situation. But I'll let him explain it."

"Shit," Rowan whispered. "He's the Arch Magus."

"The most powerful mage in the world?"

She nodded. "The very one."

I'd heard of the Arch Magus before—he had command of more magical gifts than any other Magica. *This* was him?

I couldn't say I was surprised. If not the Arch Magus, I'd have assumed he was some sort of god.

Lachlan stepped forward, his presence filling the room. All eyes were riveted on him, and if I had super hearing, I'd guess that plenty of hearts were racing.

Not mine, of course.

Though it was embarrassingly hard to forget the caress of his magic.

"There's been a theft." Lachlan's voice rolled over the room. It was rich and deep, and tinged with a Scottish accent that sent a shiver across my skin. An embarrassing shiver.

Something touched my thigh, and I looked down to see that

the sphynx, Muffin, had pressed his foot to my leg. I met his green gaze.

Get it together.

I scowled at the cat and hissed, "I have it together."

Sure you do.

I shot him a glare, then turned back to Lachlan.

Whose eyes were on me. He moved his gaze along and continued speaking. "Two days ago, I finished production of a spell that is highly dangerous. During transport to the buyer, it was stolen. My friend Decker was abducted along with it. Both need to be recovered quickly—which is why I'm here."

Man, he was short on words, parsing them out like they were made of gold. I searched his gaze for some emotion linked to his friend's abduction, but saw nothing.

And how did someone get the drop on the Arch Magus and manage to steal from him? Shouldn't this guy be strong enough to protect the stuff he made?

He certainly looked like it. And his magic felt like it.

I raised a hand, but didn't wait to be called on. Something about this guy made me throw caution to the wind. "What was the spell?"

He was being real cagey about that.

"An *ancientus* spell."

Holy fates. *Ancientus* spells could bring back magic from the past, dangerous magic that had been locked away for good reason. They were insanely rare spells. Even I'd heard of the time an *ancientus* spell had been used to bring back the Black Death. It could kill thousands if used the wrong way. Or it could save lives.

But if it had been stolen and a person kidnapped...that didn't sound like people who wanted to use it for good.

Who the hell had he been making it for?

I leaned toward Rowan and muttered, "Sounds to me like the spell never should have been made."

Lachlan's gaze lingered on me before he continued. "We have one clue about where the magic was taken. The City of Lights, The City of Invaders. But that name could be interpreted in many different ways, and so I need more help. I know that the Protectorate has the best trackers for the job, so I've made an offer to Jude and the rest of the directors."

Jude stepped forward. "We will divide up into teams. The spell could be anywhere in the world. It's stored in a crystal sphere the size of a man's fist. Each team can interpret the clue as they wish, but the one to recover the spell will be paid a prize by Lachlan. Half a million pounds."

Whew. My jaw just about hit the floor.

This spell was *that* dangerous? He had to know that the Protectorate would search for the spell for free—it was our duty. But to add that kind of incentive?

I looked at Rowan and Bree, who were equally intrigued. We'd never had that kind of money. Hell, we'd always been poor, given that we'd funneled every penny into protection charms to conceal us from the ones who hunted us.

Five hundred thousand pounds was a *lot.*

I looked down at the Cats of Catastrophe. They looked equally interested—even the goofy orange one had his eyes glued to Jude and Lachlan.

"You guys could buy a lot of fish with that kind of dough," I said.

Muffin gave a low meow of agreement, his tail quivering in delight.

I couldn't believe I was having a conversation with a cat. Especially a cat wearing an emerald earring. I turned my attention back to the front of the room, unable to look away from Lachlan.

He was riveting. And suspicious.

I listened with half an ear as Jude explained that they would divide us into teams tonight and give us our partners. *The City of Lights, the City of Invaders.* Something tugged at my mind, but I couldn't place it. It was a strange feeling though—sparkling like bubbles in my head. Weird.

When everyone got up to leave, I found myself drawn to the front of the room.

"What are you doing?" Bree hissed.

"I have a question."

"Of course. Only way to come up with plans B and C is to ask questions."

"Exactly. Gotta be prepared."

She leaned against the wall and watched. I weaved through the crowd, headed for Jude and Lachlan. As if he could sense me, he turned.

When he pinned me with his dark gaze, I almost regretted my boldness. Almost.

3

I stopped in front of him, far enough away that I didn't have to crane my neck to meet his gaze. I tried to breathe shallowly and not inhale the delicious scent of his magic—or of him.

"You're the one with the questions," he said.

"That's me." I grinned, but couldn't help the flip-flopping in my stomach. I could *feel* the tension between us. The attraction was so obvious—on my part, at least—that I could cut it with a knife. "And I have a few more."

He didn't smile, but I thought he wanted to. It would have been a devastatingly handsome twist of his lips, I was sure. "What might those be?"

"Who was your buyer for such dangerous magic? Isn't it illegal to make spells like that? Some magic has been left in the past for a reason."

"True enough, but I was making it for the Order of the Magica."

I swallowed hard at the mention of the magical government. They oversaw Magica—magic users like me. The Shifter Council was in charge of all other supernaturals. Those who *were* magic as opposed to those who *used* it.

Unfortunately, the Order of the Magica didn't like my kind very much. Dragon Gods were so powerful, we were considered dangerous. We upset the natural balance of things. I needed the backing of a powerful organization like the Undercover Protectorate if I wanted a life that didn't involve being on the run all the time.

"And you're the Arch Magus."

"I am."

"So how did they get the drop on you?"

His right brow arched. "You think that I'm running some kind of con? That they didn't really steal the spell?"

"A lot of people want to get within these walls." I gestured to the walls of the room, but I really meant the entire Protectorate castle. We carefully guarded our turf. "And you're supposed to be insanely powerful, right? More magical gifts than any other supernatural?"

He nodded curtly. "Twelve gifts."

"And you couldn't use those to protect your spell?"

"There were twenty-five in the ambush. I took out twelve. Then they took my friend Decker hostage. I couldn't risk his life."

"Hmmm. One for each gift."

"You think you could do better?"

"Maybe." Okay, that was a big fat lie. Without the Cats of Catastrophe, six demons would have gotten me tonight.

"Where do you think the clue leads?" he asked.

My mind raced, buzzing with energy. It was a strange feeling, totally unfamiliar, and I stifled a gasp. Pain flared, making my eyes water, and unfamiliar magic flowed through me. But then the name of a city blazed in my mind.

Paris.

Follow it.

The instructions sounded in my mind, spoken by a voice not my own.

I'd asked a question, and it had answered.

Paris. I'd never been more certain of anything.

"Paris." I choked out the word.

His gaze sharpened. "Why?"

Around us, the room emptied, people flowing out to get back to bed for a few hours. But I had eyes only for him. My mind buzzed, but he was all I could see. I couldn't tell him that magic had told me, however. I was supposed to be a shield mage. Not a prophet or seer. New powers didn't just develop for most supernaturals.

They did for Dragon Gods, but I certainly couldn't tell him that.

My mind scrambled for a justification for Paris. "Lots of lights. And the Romans founded it. The most famous invaders in history."

Hey, that was pretty good. It was even true.

"You like history?" he asked.

"Sure." Not quite true. I liked art, and art often portrayed history. But that wasn't why I'd chosen Paris.

"There are over three dozen cites known as the City of Lights." He gave me an appraising look. "But you chose Paris."

"Yep." I shook away my nerves over the strange new magic and focused on him. "And I'm right about it, too."

"Confident."

"Always." It was cocky, but a positive attitude had carried me through life. It left no time for wimping out. Sure, I had my doubts about myself and my magic, but that wouldn't stop me from powering through. Or at least trying to.

And I *was* confident about this.

I felt it in my bones.

He cocked his head, staring hard at me. As if he were trying to see through me. I fidgeted, then forced myself still.

"Seen enough?" I asked.

"You're special," he said. "Something about your magic."

I shrugged. "Garden variety shield mage here."

"No one at the Protectorate is garden variety."

"Oh, you haven't seen me fight yet."

The corner of his full lips quirked up in a sexy smile. "I'd like to."

I swallowed hard. Yep, this was above my pay grade. Flirting with sexy super mages was not my usual activity. My usual was dumb movies and Cheezy Puffs. Or if I was feeling fancy, cheap champagne and my painting.

"What about you is so special?" he asked.

"Um." Well, hell. "I can run a six-minute mile, and I'm good with cars. Like, real good."

"That's not what I mean."

"I know. I just don't have anything else." *Except for the fact that I'm a Dragon God.* And yeah, not sharing that right now. My powers hadn't developed, and I didn't even know what pantheon I was. Until I knew that, saying I was a late-blooming half-developed supernatural didn't interest me. What if I never mastered my power at all? Maybe it was my weak spot—always worrying about being behind Bree—but I wanted to keep that to myself.

"And you're dangerous," he said.

"Well, considering that I can kick ass in six languages, that goes without saying."

"Not just the fighting." He nodded his head, clearly having decided something. "We'll work together on this."

"Wha—" My jaw dropped open, and I looked around. "I don't get it."

"Everyone pairs up on this. I want to work with you. There's something about you."

"Not a guess. I know."

"Exactly. It's settled."

I frowned. "Do I still qualify for the prize?"

"Aye. And you don't even have to split it."

I liked the sound of that. Last thing I wanted was to get paired up with Lavender and have to split with her.

From behind him, Jude caught my eye. I shot her a *holy crap, what do I do?* look, trying to keep it subtle.

She approached, stopping at Lachlan's side. "I think it's a brilliant plan."

"You do?"

"Indeed. It'll give you a chance to practice your skills."

I nodded. "Right. Of course."

Lachlan smiled. "It's settled, then. I'll see you in the morning. Eight a.m, the front entry."

I nodded dumbly, watching him turn and walk away, then I looked at Jude. "You really think this is a good idea?"

"You need to get out in the real world. Training here isn't doing you any favors."

"No, it's not."

"You're good in the real world, Ana. Your fighting skills are off the charts. I don't know why you're floundering at the Academy, but clearly you need a change of scenery. If you can find this spell, it'll go a long way toward helping you make it through the Academy."

"So I don't get kicked out."

"Exactly." She frowned. "We really don't want that. We want you here with us. But you have to pass."

I gulped. Fates, I wanted that, too.

"Rules are rules," Jude said. "And Arach is serious about them. I can't go against her."

Arach, the dragon spirit who had built this place, rarely showed up. But when she did, it was like getting hit in the face with raw power. I needed her approval to stay here. And boy, did I want to stay here with my sisters. Stay in this amazing castle where I could have a life doing good. Where I wasn't hunted for what I was. And since the alternative was getting kicked out on my butt, alone, I had some really good motivation.

"If it's so important to find this spell, could we ask the Fire-Souls for help?" I asked.

The FireSouls were our friends from years ago. Like us, they were hunted for their magic. Each FireSoul had inherited the soul of a dragon, and it allowed them to find anything of value. Treasure, basically. Dragons loved treasure. They could find this thing. They kept their true species a secret from most, but Jude knew what they were.

"He already asked," she said. "They're busy with an emergency."

"Bigger than this?"

"Apparently."

"Whew." That had to be something. "But he knows them? And what they are?"

"No," Jude said. "I asked for him. As soon as he came to me, I went to them to see if we could freelance their services. But it was a no-go. At least not at the moment."

"We'll find it," I said. "I'll do whatever it takes. I'll team up with Lachlan. And I'll find that damned spell. Then will I graduate?"

"No." She smiled. "But it'll help."

"Good."

She squeezed my arm, a friendly gesture that warmed me. She was way too young to seem like a mom, but ever since we'd lost our mother, my sisters and I seemed to seek out motherly-type affection just about anywhere we could find it.

Not that I'd tell her that. Too weird.

"Thanks, Jude."

"Good luck, Ana."

I had a feeling I was going to need it.

Bree, Rowan, and I walked back to our apartments without talking. The Cats of Catastrophe followed along in silence. We passed through hallways and corridors, some done up in grand style and others as ancient-looking as if they had been in the thirteenth century.

We each had a tower apartment at the back of the massive castle, and Bree and Rowan followed me through the door into mine, up the winding staircase, and into the main entry room.

"You're going to have to spill, you know," Bree said.

"I know, I know." I watched the Cats of Catastrophe saunter to my couch.

Muffin and Bojangles jumped right up to make themselves comfortable, but Princess Snowflake III knocked over a large pillow then leapt onto it, settling her fluffy white butt right onto the soft surface.

"I put my face on that sometimes, you know," I said.

She just glared at me, green eyes glinting.

"All right, all right." I raised my hands and turned toward the kitchen. The large round space was the living room, kitchen, and dining room in one, with a bedroom up above, accessed by an iron spiral staircase.

The whole apartment was decorated in beautiful, classy neutrals. It'd been an empty space when I'd first walked into it three months ago, but magic had allowed it to see into my psyche and had somehow decorated it in a manner to suit me.

Honestly, the classy look surprised me. I'd spent most of my life as a low-level outlaw, just trying to survive, or as a desert rat driving a monster truck across Death Valley, transporting criminals to Hider's Haven, a place where they could hide out from the law.

The fact that the magical apartment thought I was all classy and crap was a surprise to me. I liked to paint, though, putting crazy splashes of color on canvas. For the first time in my life, these last three months at the Undercover Protectorate had given me the time and safety to work, and several of my paintings livened up the space. They weren't great, but I liked them. And seeing my easel and paints set up on the other side of the room always gave me a warm little glow.

This was a real life here. One with a real home instead of a shack, and hobbies instead of constantly hiding. Friends instead of loneliness.

I wanted to keep this.

"Getting drinks?" Bree asked.

"Yeah." I opened the fridge. "Champagne all right with you?"

"Pink kind?" Bree asked.

"Sure." I grabbed a glass bottle full of pale pink liquid. It was cheap champagne—all of it was—but anything with bubbles suited me, and I wasn't picky.

I popped the cork, poured some, and handed out the glasses.

Rowan glanced at the full couch, then at the table. "Better sit there."

I glanced at the cats. All three of them looked up from licking their butts, and it was clear that they weren't about to move. "Yeah, definitely."

I sat and sipped my drink, enjoying the pop of bubbles on my tongue.

Rowan took a sip and cringed. "I don't know how you drink this stuff."

"Hey, hey, Miss Fancy Tastes, it's not that bad."

Bree sipped hers. "Yeah, I like it."

"You only like it because it's pink," Rowan said.

Bree grinned widely, her teeth glinting in the light. "True enough."

Bree was a hardcore badass, chewing up demons for breakfast and not even spitting out the bones. Which made her love of froufrou pink cocktails even funnier.

She turned to me, eyes going serious. "Now spill. I tried to listen in on your conversation with Lachlan, but he used some kind of blocking spell."

My brows rose. "Really?"

Bree was the Valkyrie Dragon God, and as such, she'd been gifted with the powers of multiple Viking gods. One of those powers was incredible hearing, given to her by Heimdall, a Norse god.

If I ever got my act together and made my transition to Dragon God, some mysterious pantheon of ancient gods would give me their powers as well. Theoretically, at least.

"Spill," Bree said.

I shook my head, realizing I'd drifted off a bit. "Sorry. Yeah. Well, I'm going to team up with him to solve this. He liked my theory that the spell was taken to Paris, and he thinks I'm interesting—dangerous, actually—so he wants to work with me."

"Uh-oh," Bree said. "I don't like the sound of that. _He_ looks dangerous."

"He also looked kinda hot." Rowan raised her brows at me, clearly waiting for me to agree.

I nodded. "Yeah. Mega hot."

"Mega dangerous," Bree said. "And cold. I could feel the self-control wafting off him."

"You're just in love with Cade, so you don't have eyes for anyone else," I said.

"She's right about the self-control, though. That dude is tightly wound."

I wouldn't mind unwinding him.

No! Bad Ana! Down girl.

"Agreed." I sipped, remembering the lethal strength coiled in his large body, and the dark knowing in his eyes. *What* he knew, I couldn't quite pinpoint. But it made me want to shiver, and not because Bree and Rowan thought he was cold.

Far from it.

"Why Paris?" Bree asked.

"City of Lights, City of Invaders." I explained the theory about the Romans. "But really, I just had a feeling. Something took me over and *told* me it was Paris."

Rowan frowned. "*Told* you?"

"Yeah. It felt like magic, guys. Something I wasn't in control of. It spoke in my mind, telling me to follow my instinct. I asked a question, and it answered."

Bree leaned forward, eyes wide. "Is it your Dragon God powers coming to life?"

I touched the back of my neck, where a four-pointed star existed. I'd been born with the Mark of Power. All three of us had one, though we hid them with magic. If I hadn't had the mark, I would have doubted I was a Dragon God. Was this it? Finally? "Maybe."

Bree chewed her lip. "I bet it is. That's how it happened with me."

"So your new power is just *knowing*?" Rowan asked.

"Maybe? Prophecy or premonition or something."

"That could be any pantheon," Bree said.

But which one would choose *me*?

"You've got to learn to master your new power," Bree said. "Control it. Or it will devour you. Body and mind."

I swallowed hard, dread spreading through me.

Bree knew from experience, as it had happened to her. She'd even lost one of her powers as a result. She'd been too slow to adapt and had lost her power to throw sonic booms.

The transition was the scariest part of being a Dragon God. I wanted it to happen—it *had* to happen, or I'd fail the Academy and be out on my ass.

But it was going to be really freaking difficult. As new powers developed, they went out of control inside the Dragon God. If I couldn't learn to control them, I'd end up losing all my magic. Which was like losing my soul.

Then I'd be so damned miserable I'd just want to curl up and die. I'd seen it happen before—it was a terrible fate.

"Has your magic been acting up in any other ways?" Bree asked.

"No. Not since that time last month, when the weird white light glowed from me." We'd been in the middle of a terrible journey across a wasteland. Sickness wraiths had almost killed us, but I'd suddenly started to glow with a light that had repelled them. We'd thought it might be my Dragon God magic coming alive, but it had never happened again. "Just the one little premonition."

"Be alert, then," Bree said. "The change could be coming. And you'll have to be ready."

"Be careful." Rowan's eyes gleamed with worry. "We're here for you if you need us."

I nodded absentmindedly, getting up to go to the window. It was dark outside, but a full moon shed a bright glow over the amazing landscape.

I couldn't believe I lived here. I loved it. This amazing place was my *home*. For all our life, we'd been hunted by an unknown threat that had killed our mother. We'd hidden from them for years, broke and scared. They were the ultimate bogeyman.

With the help of the Undercover Protectorate, we'd finally destroyed them. And here, we'd found a real home—a place where we were safe and could do good work. A place I loved.

I just had to make sure I didn't lose it.

4

Of course I woke up to the sight of a cat's butt right in my face. Bojangles turned around and looked at me, his little tongue lolling out of his mouth.

"Ugh." I nudged him aside, and he flopped down and meowed, rubbing his head against my hand.

"Good morning to you, too." A smile stretched across my face.

I completed my quick morning ritual under the watchful gazes of three cats. Since there was a carnage of ham bones on the kitchen counter, I had to assume that they'd fed themselves, probably with the help of Mayhem, the ghostly pug who followed Bree everywhere. Hams were Mayhem's favorite, and Hans, the cook, seemed to have an endless supply of them.

Muffin, the scraggly hairless cat who sat on the counter, burped, his whiskers quivering. I laughed. I should've been annoyed about the mess, but I'd always wanted a pet. Our lives had been too barren before now to have one.

I gave Muffin a serious look. "Clean up after yourself."

He meowed. *Who, me? But I'm just a cat without opposable thumbs!*

He even held up a paw.

"If you can run jewel heists, you can clean up your ham bones."

Fine.

"Thank you." I threw on a leather jacket and headed to the door. "And don't wreck anything while I'm gone."

Princess Snowflake III hissed, but the other two meowed their agreement.

My boots thudded on the stairs as I made my way down the tower. It was only a minute to eight, so I picked up the pace, racing through the old stone corridor and skipping down the wide, sweeping staircase.

Lachlan waited for me in the courtyard outside, the wind ruffling his dark hair. His dark eyes zeroed in on me, making me feel like a bug under glass.

But somehow, I didn't hate it.

His attention might make me a bit nervous, but I found I *wanted* it. Probably because he was checking me out. From the way his gaze subtly covered my whole form, he was *definitely* checking me out.

The sun gleamed on him, highlighting the tightly leashed power that he possessed. His eyes glinted, almost cold, like Bree had said.

Not cold enough for me, though. He was dangerous, but I could get on board with that.

No! That was dumb and risky.

Better to play it distant and safe.

I slowed to a walk as I approached, my stomach full of flutters.

"Ready?" I asked.

He nodded.

A man of few words. I could work with that. More time for me to talk. And up close, his eyes weren't cold. They were just blank. His face carefully controlled to show no expression.

"How are we getting to Paris?" I asked.

He didn't answer, just held out his hand, palm forward. His magic swelled on the air, the scent of pine and the taste of caramel. I shivered at the feel of a caress, and watched as a gleaming silver light appeared in front of his palm. The light grew, becoming five feet tall and three wide. Then bigger.

"Holy fates, you can make a portal?" I demanded.

"Aye."

I whistled. That was some *rare* magic. I'd never met a single Magica who could do that—and I'd even met a few gods in my day. I gave him an appreciative look.

He gestured for me to step through, so I did.

The ether sucked me in, sending me on a topsy-turvy ride through space. Darkness swirled, then the portal spit me out into the gloom of a stormy day.

Paris in the rain.

It poured from above. The sky was a tumultuous gray that suggested the only reasonable place to be was in bed. It was so dark that it appeared to be dusk.

Just our luck.

I shivered and stepped aside.

Lachlan appeared a moment later, right in the place where I'd been standing. A scowl creased his face. "Bloody hell."

"Should have checked the weather." I popped my leather collar up, but it didn't do much to protect me from the cold rain.

"No need." He waved a hand overhead, and a little clearing appeared.

The rain no longer pattered coldly on my cheeks, but it splashed into puddles just a few feet away. He'd created a clearing around us, protecting us from the rain.

"Wow. You control weather?" I asked.

"In small bits." He gestured around. "Stopping a rainstorm around all of Paris is a bit above my pay grade, but I can handle this."

I wiped the water from my cheeks. "Good. I like it."

"Any idea where to go next?" His gaze studied me assessingly, waiting.

Suddenly, the bug-under-glass sensation didn't feel so great.

I reached for my new magic, having no idea how to access or control it.

It lay dormant within me.

Was it even a new power?

I had no freaking idea. But it had quit working on me. "The spell you made packs some serious punch, right? So if there's someone in town who keeps track of powerful new magic coming into town, they might be able to help us."

Lachlan nodded. "If the spell actually is here, then Madame Alamedra might know."

"Who is she?"

"A ghost at Père Lachaise."

"The big cemetery?" Even I had heard of the massive cemetery in the middle of Paris. Mostly because it had one of the most active supernatural neighborhoods in all of Europe.

"The same. She knows all of the magical goings-on in the city, and if there's something new here, she'll know how to find it."

"All right. Lead on."

He nodded and turned, heading down the street with a quick stride. I hurried to keep up. His damned long legs were hard to match pace with, but I was determined to try, since the magical rain shield was only around him. Neither did I want to be a drag, slowing him down.

We cut through the bustling city. The streets were fairly empty, and much darker than usual, but still beautiful. I'd never been to France. I'd never been most places, unless it was to help Bree fight some bad guys.

I searched the skyline for the Eiffel Tower, but it was concealed in the clouds and rain.

"This way." Lachlan waved for me to follow, and we turned to cross the street.

We darted in front of gleaming yellow headlights, stopping near a massive stone arch at the entrance of the cemetery.

"Whoa." I craned my neck to look upward. "Only fancy people buried here."

"For the most part. This is the supernatural section. Blocked from human tourists."

"They can't see it?"

"Precisely. And they're directed away by other pressing matters."

Like the Undercover Protectorate's castle. It was a handy magic.

Lachlan walked up to the heavy iron gate that blocked our way through the arch. I followed, shuddering at the magic that raced over my skin. It stung like the bite of fire ants.

"Holy fates." I rubbed my arms, wincing. "Supernaturals aren't welcome either."

"Not without invitation, no."

I debated using my shield magic, but didn't want to waste it. I could take a little pain.

Lachlan sucked in a deep breath, then pressed his hand to the heavy iron gate. A sizzling noise sounded, and the air around his palm seemed to smoke slightly. He winced and pushed the door open.

Holy fates, it was burning his hand.

"Go." His voice was rough.

I darted through the gate, and he followed, shaking his hand.

The path into the cemetery stretched ahead of us, bordered

on both sides by small crypts and towering trees. It seemed darker in here, and colder, as if it were nighttime.

The air crackled with protective magic, still burning my skin. I hurried forward to get past the protective barrier.

Within ten feet, the feeling faded, and I sighed.

The air exploded with motion. Figures lunged out from one of the crypts, their claws outstretched for us.

I flung out my hand, calling on my magic and blasting my shield outward.

It exploded in a flash of white, creating a barrier between us and the creatures.

"That's handy," Lachlan said.

Panting, I studied our attackers. There were six of them, and all looked to be in various states of decay.

"Zombies?" I asked.

"Revenants. They're similar. They guard the cemetery from visitors without an invitation. We have to convince them to let us pass."

"Convince?"

They hissed and clawed at my protective shield, their skin peeling off their muscles and flashes of white bone peeking through. They stank like death and decay, making my eyes water.

I shivered.

"Fight," Lachlan said.

"Yeah, that's about what I—"

My shield faltered and died. Panic stabbed me as the revenants lunged forward, their mouths gaping open.

Instinct took over. I called two daggers from the ether, gripping one in either hand, then flung them toward the closest revenants. They plunged into the beasts' necks, sending them flying backward.

The creatures stumbled to the ground, but the other four leapt forward.

Lachlan drew two short swords from the ether—they were more like massive daggers, really. He sprang for the nearest revenant, crossing both blades and dragging them across the creature's neck like scissors. The head toppled to the ground, and the body followed.

All right, then.

I drew a sword from the ether. It wasn't my preferred weapon, but I was handy with it. I was handy with all weapons, actually.

Someone with my wimpy magic had to be.

A revenant with one eye was nearly on me, so close I could smell its fetid breath. I swung my sword, going for the neck. It sliced through cleanly, and I thanked my lucky stars I'd saved up for the expensive steel.

As the head tumbled to the ground, I kicked out and sent the body flying after it. Then I whirled and struck out at another revenant, taking his head just as quickly.

Next to me, Lachlan moved so fast that he was a blur. Revenant heads flew, and within seconds, they were all down.

He turned to me, not a hair out of place. His breathing hadn't even changed. His gaze surveyed the three revenants at my feet. "Well done."

"Thanks." But I couldn't enjoy the praise.

My shield had died.

My magic was acting up. That had to be part of the transition to Dragon God.

Please don't notice.

"But we'd better get a move on." He nodded at something on the ground, and I looked down.

A revenant body was crawling toward a head. "Ah crap."

"Come on." He waited for me to come, then followed.

"How long until they put themselves back together?"

"Not long, but they won't be our problem at that point. We just have to get away from the gate. Once we're out of their turf, they can't sense us."

"These ghosts sure are picky about who visits."

"They like a little warning, at least."

As soon as he said it, I swore I felt eyes on me. I peered around. Rain poured on the headstones and crypts that surrounded the path, weighing down the trees' leaves. Puddles gleamed in the grass. A hazy mist lay heavy on the ground, but my eyes were drawn toward the trees.

I squinted, catching sight of little gleaming lights.

Eyes.

"Someone is watching us," I murmured. I gripped my sword more tightly.

"Bats. They have ghostly masters who can see through their eyes."

"Great." I swallowed hard. I liked a challenge, but if all the ghosts in this cemetery decided they didn't want us here, we'd be hard-pressed to make it out. "Can you make a portal out of here?"

"Thinking up a quick escape?"

"Maybe."

"Unfortunately, no. This place is guarded."

"Dang."

Noise sounded from up above, and lights cut through the gloom. I picked up my pace, but kept my senses alert.

Soon, the graveyard came alive. It was as if we'd stepped onto a ghostly city street. All the figures were shades of transparent blue-gray, and dressed in clothes from at least three centuries. The free-standing crypts and mausoleums had their doors swung wide. I peeked inside, realizing that they'd been turned into shops and bars, restaurants and salons.

"This is amazing," I murmured.

"Biggest ghost city in the world."

A woman wearing a fantastically huge ball gown looked at me, and then her gaze darted to Lachlan. She smiled and gestured him closer, a come-hither look in her eyes.

I didn't know what she thought she was going to accomplish with a guy who wasn't a ghost, but if I were her, I'd probably try it, too.

Lachlan inclined his head politely, and kept walking. We passed by street merchants hawking their wares—ghostly clothing and food, mostly—as well as street musicians and patrolmen on ghostly horses. They looked like old-timey cops. But dead.

The patrolmen looked at us from beneath the brims of their hats, their eyes glowing a bright green.

"They're the ones who see through the bats' eyes?" I whispered.

"Aye."

Lachlan raised a hand in a subtle greeting, and the patrolmen nodded.

"They know you?"

"I come here occasionally." He stopped and ducked through the low doorway of a large mausoleum.

I followed, stepping into a raucous nightclub from the early twentieth century. Or maybe the late nineteenth. I wasn't an expert, but the decor and clothes were *old*. There were chorus girls, though, the fancy French kind with the ruffled skirts that flared high as they kicked their legs toward the ceiling.

A skinny ghost with a top hat banged away at an old piano as the revelers swilled glasses of gleaming green liquid. The air of the place was jovial, but a few turned to glare at us.

"They don't always like the living," Lachlan murmured.

"Oh, I don't know. Doesn't seem so bad to be dead."

"They've created something nice here, but some still want to leave."

I could understand. I didn't like being stuck either. I edged closer to Lachlan as we made our way toward the bar. Ghosts were tricky in a fight. Nearly impossible to destroy since they were already dead, and some of them still had their magic.

Which put *us* at a distinct disadvantage.

There were a few figures leaning against the bar, and Lachlan chose to approach a chorus girl. A cigarette dangled from her fingertips, and her eyes glowed with a similar light as she watched him approach.

I might as well have not existed, which was probably for the best. I lingered in the shadows, just close enough to hear, and let him get down to it.

Lachlan leaned against the bar and smiled. "Hello, Marlena."

"Lachlan. It's been too long. " Her French accent was thick and her eyes hot as they traveled up and down his form.

"Far too long."

"What do you want now?"

"Just a bit of information, love."

I bristled at the endearment, then mentally kicked myself. *Idiot.* Now was not the time to get possessive over some dude I'd just met. *Never* was actually the appropriate time for that.

"Ah, the usual." She frowned and crossed her arms over her chest. "What for?"

"Decker is missing."

Concern glinted in her eyes, and her lips softened. "What happened?"

"Abducted by someone who stole some dangerous magic from me."

"Silly Lachlan, still crafting such deadly tricks."

"They pay well."

She harrumphed. "What do you need?" She shook her finger. "And I'm only helping you for Marcus's sake, just so you're aware."

"I am. I need to know where Madam Alamedra is."

"Ah, but of course. I heard that she is at the pond tonight, performing some silly spell."

"You know they aren't silly."

She shrugged. "In the eye of the beholder."

His face shifted into an expression that was almost kind. There was a hint of caring at least, something I hadn't yet seen on his face. I watched, undeniably envious and hating myself for it, as he picked up her hand and kissed the back of it.

I didn't know if he actually moved her hand, or if she did. I'd never touched a ghost before. The mechanics of it were a mystery.

But she smiled, then shooed him away.

He joined me again, leaning low to murmur against my ear. "Ready to go?"

I shivered at the warmth of his breath. "Yep."

I stepped away, not sure why he chose that moment to stand so close. His gaze lingered on mine just before he turned and led the way out of the bar. I followed him onto the street, my gaze darting all around the ghostly city as we walked. It was one of the most fascinating places I'd ever been, and I wanted to bring Rowan and Bree back here.

"What is Madame Alamedra?" I asked.

"She's a seer. Ancient."

"Perfect." Age often equaled power.

The cemetery sloped downhill toward a pond. At the edge, fireflies danced in the rain, circling around a woman wearing a flowing cape that twirled in the wind. She was doing some kind of strange dance, and humming low in her throat. As we stepped off the path and onto the grass, she stopped dead, then turned.

Her dark eyes burned me. I flinched, but there was no getting away. She was looking into my soul.

I sure hoped she liked what she found.

"Reading the future?" Lachlan asked as we approached.

She cackled, and up close, I could see that she looked older. She'd lived a long, full life before she'd become a ghost.

"I'm dancing, you nitwit. The fireflies needed a partner, and so did I."

I smiled.

"What are you smiling at, girlie?" she demanded.

"Um. You?"

She nodded. "All right, then."

"We need your help, Madame Alamedra," Lachlan said.

"Of course you do. What is it this time?"

He explained about the missing magic and his friend Decker.

Madame Alamedra sighed. "When will you stop with this dangerous magic, Lachlan?"

"Probably never." He grinned. "I'm the only one capable of making it."

"Perhaps it should stay unmade."

"Impossible. But will you help us?"

She sighed. "Yes. But for a price."

"What?"

"You will owe me a favor. A dangerous one. And you must come back and dance with me and the fireflies. You're stealing their partner for the night, and they don't appreciate it."

A pained expression crossed his face. He really didn't seem like the dancing-with-fireflies type. "That's two favors."

"I don't care."

His mouth thinned.

"I'll do it," I said. "I'll dance with you and the fireflies."

I wanted to come back here sometime, to see more of it. And

I liked Madame Alamedra. Not to mention, how often did one get to dance with fireflies in a graveyard city? Not often. Hardly ever, even.

Madame Alamedra looked at me, her sharp eyes assessing. Then she nodded. "All right, then. At a time of my choosing."

"Okay."

"This way." She waved her hand for us to follow, and hurried up the slope toward the path.

Lachlan joined me as we walked, leaning down to whisper, "Thank you."

"I could tell you weren't that keen on it. And I am." I glanced at him.

He was shooting me an evaluating gaze, then he hurried to keep up with Madame Alamedra.

She led us to a large building at the very edge of the ghostly part of town. I could feel the magic fading as we neared the human part of the graveyard.

"Here we are." She drifted through a large door.

Lachlan pushed it open for us, and we walked inside.

The space was pitch-black, so I raised my hand, igniting the magic in my lightstone ring. It had been a gift from my old friends the FireSouls.

The light flared, illuminating hundreds of shelves all over the walls. Bones were stacked in them, all in piles. Millions and millions of bones.

"What is this place?" I spun in a circle, taking it all in. There were some statues here and there, along with a soaring ceiling, but for the most part, it was just bones.

"The ossuary," Lachlan said. "The cemetery gets too full, so they dig up the bodies eventually and put them here."

"Good for my work." Madame Alamedra cackled. "They make it easy for me!"

She raised her hands, and magic swelled on the air. It

smelled of fresh bread and sounded like the tinkling of wind chimes. The bones flew off the shelf, whirling around in the air like a cyclone. I ducked, narrowly avoiding being hit by a leg bone.

Madame Alamedra continued to laugh, clearly liking her work. I stayed crouched low, and Lachlan joined me. The bones slowed, forming a pattern.

"Ah, yes." Madame Alamedra sighed. "But of course."

"Of course what?" I had no idea what the heck she saw in the bones. They were still just swirling in the air, totally unrecognizable in pattern.

But they kept moving and soon, the Eiffel Tower appeared. Magic made my skin prickle.

"Holy fates," I murmured. These bones were smart.

Madame Alamedra murmured something unintelligible, then flung her hands downward. The magic on the air faded, and the bones zipped back to their places on the shelves, leaving the room silent.

Slowly, I rose.

Madame Alamedra turned, her eyes glinting. "It looks like you must borrow my crystal."

"I promise to return it," Lachlan said.

"What's going on?" I asked.

"The Eiffel Tower is more than just a monument," Madame Alamedra said. "It is a magical beacon. An indicator. Because the bones revealed it just now, it means that there is new, dangerous magic in the city." Her gaze riveted to Lachlan. "The magic you seek, perhaps."

"And the crystal?" I asked.

"It will help focus the tower's energy and lead you to where the magic is located. You must climb the tower and place the crystal at the top. Watch out for the guards. When the sun or moonlight strikes it, it will reveal the location of the magic."

"Climb the Eiffel Tower." My voice was weak. I did *not* like heights.

"Is that a problem?" Lachlan asked.

"Nope!" My voice definitely squeaked. "I love climbing big monuments. High into the sky."

"Liar." But his voice was soft. Almost tender. The corner of his mouth tugged up. I couldn't call it a smile, but I did like it.

"Whatever. Let's go do it."

Madame Alamedra smiled. "Remember your vow."

I saluted. "One dance, coming right up."

5

We left the cemetery the same way we'd come in, but this time, we headed right down the street instead of crossing. When an old-fashioned-looking streetcar passed by, traveling via electrified wires, Lachlan jumped aboard the back, hanging onto the handrail.

He reached back for me, holding out a hand. It was a snapshot of a romantic moment from a movie.

But it was real life, and we were hunting bad guys.

I shook away the silly thought and grabbed his hand. His touch sent an electric frisson up my arm as he swung me up. I gripped the rail of the streetcar and clung on.

The streetcar zipped through the bustling streets, cutting through the rain. Lights from the shops whipped by, and the day was darker than ever. It was early winter, and the sun was setting.

I shivered in my coat.

A few more people jumped on, hanging to the rails. Lachlan was forced closer to me, the warm length of his body pressed against my back. He towered over me, and I squeezed my eyes shut. I was intensely aware of every inch of him, this near stranger who seemed so cold but sometimes looked at me with heat in his eyes.

Eventually, the Eiffel Tower appeared on the horizon, spearing up through the sky.

"We'll get off here." Lachlan leapt down, and I followed.

He looked at his watch. "We need to kill an hour until the tower closes and it becomes dark. Are you hungry?"

My stomach growled. "Always."

We found a small, warm cafe and hustled inside. It was bustling and busy, but we managed to snag a table near the window. One with a perfect view of the Eiffel Tower.

We ordered tiny coffees and impressive sandwiches on beautiful baguettes. My first bite tasted like heaven. Lachlan ate his while watching me.

"Why are you looking at me like I'm a bug under glass?"

"I'm trying to figure out what you are. What's so special about you."

Great. "I'm a trainee at the Academy."

"They don't take just anyone."

"True enough. But I'm not keen on sharing the details with you."

"Playing it close to the vest?"

"A woman's got to have some secrets." I wasn't about to spill my secrets to a guy I hardly knew. Until I knew what pantheon I was—until I had control of my magic—I'd be keeping that info to myself.

Interest flashed in his eyes. He reached for a napkin, and his hand brushed mine. Heat flashed up my arm, and my gaze darted to his.

Fire burned in his eyes. He drew his hand back and cleared his throat, clearly trying to get back on track. "Why did your shield falter back at the entrance to the cemetery? I can sense that you're strong. It shouldn't have died so quickly."

Damn. He had noticed. I shrugged. "Sometimes it's finicky."
Lie.

"Hmmm." He finished off his sandwich.

"Well, what about you? You're super special. How'd you get so many magical gifts?" Most mages had one. A few were born with as many as four. Twelve? It was unheard of.

"Just lucky, I guess."

I was beginning to hate that word—*special.* We were both being cagey, though, and it just made me want to learn more about him. He clearly wasn't used to sharing, and neither was I.

I'd never met a guy who had me so interested and so on edge all at the same time. I forced myself back on topic. "Your friend was abducted along with the spell."

Pain flashed briefly in his eyes, then shuttered. "We'll get him back. Decker doesn't deserve this for helping me."

I was intrigued by him. By the pain he tried to hide, and the cold front he presented to the world. But he wasn't cold at all. He wouldn't let people see what he felt, but he *did* feel. "No one deserves to be abducted for any reason."

"No, they don't."

"Do you regret making the spell?"

"I will if we don't get it back." His shoulders were tight. "Otherwise, it's my job. I'm one of the few mages powerful enough to create such magic, and in the right hands, it can make the world a better place."

"We'll get it back." I polished off the last bite of my sandwich.

He stood and put some money on the table, and I followed him out into the night. It was still early, but the continuing storm made it as dark as midnight and emptied the streets. We hurried across the road to the lawn that surrounded the tower.

Magic pricked against my skin as we stepped onto the grass. "Another protective spell?"

"Aye. It'll alert the guards."

"What kind of guards?"

He pointed into the distance. Three massive figures galloped toward us. I squinted through the gloom, trying to see what they were. Red eyes blazed at us. Through the mist, giant dogs appeared, a hundred yards away.

"Oh crap! Hellhounds?"

"The very same."

I shuddered. No way I wanted to mess with them. "They must be hell on the tourists."

"Tourists can't see them. Only supernaturals. Because the tower is so magical, all sorts of our kind want to use it for various purposes. The city council put the guards on it to minimize use."

"How do we get past them?"

They were picking up speed, only fifty yards away now.

"Try to outrun them." He started to run.

"Great." I followed, heart thundering as I neared the dogs.

The smell of brimstone preceded them, rolling across the ground, and their fangs gleamed in the light. Not all hellhounds were evil or mean—but they sure did make great guard dogs when they put their mind to it.

And these three hulking beasts were *determined.*

Two of them went for Lachlan, which really was smart, since he was so big and so fast, and one headed straight for me. One was about all I was prepared to handle, anyway.

No lie, I liked to be the toughest one in a fight, but I had nothing to prove to Lachlan or the hellhounds. Especially if it meant making it out of here alive.

I darted left as the hellhound neared, barely dodging his fangs. His growl sent a shiver through me, and I picked up the pace, racing toward the tower. I could feel the thunder of his footsteps through the ground, and my skin chilled.

I looked behind me, catching sight of his gleaming red eyes just feet away.

Shit!

I raced ahead, darting left and right, trying to stay just out of reach of his fangs. This was *not* going well. The tower was still thirty yards way.

Something heavy slammed into my back, and I plowed into the grass, skidding on my hands and knees. My panic flared, then died under the cold calm that came when instinct kicked in. I flipped over, kicking up with my legs, throwing the hellhound off of me.

It took all my strength, but the beast flew through the air, landed against the ground, and scrambled upright.

I drew my sword from the ether, but hated the idea of hurting the hellhound. He might be a hell beast, but he was still a dog. Killing him would be awful—if I even *could*. It was nearly impossible to kill the monsters.

I held out the blade. "You watch it, doggy, or I'll send you back to hell."

The beast growled and lunged. I held out my blade. If he wanted to run into it, he could.

A flash appeared from the corner of my vision. Three tiny blurs raced at the hellhound, slamming into his side.

The Cats of Catastrophe!

They hissed like demons, a frenzy of claws and fangs. Even Bojangles, the goofy one, had his act together. And Princess Snowflake III! She went for the eyes, of course.

"Thanks, guys!" I spun and ran, leaving them to take care of the hellhound. He was a big beast, but the Cats of Catastrophe were some seriously tough felines.

Wind tore at my hair as I sprinted for the tower, joining Lachlan, who now ran without any beasts on his tail. I glanced behind to see the two hellhounds lying on the grass.

"Knocked their heads together." He panted, moving so fast I could hardly keep up. "They'll be all right."

"I can't say the same for mine." I looked behind to see the hellhound racing off, the Cats of Catastrophe hot on his heels.

"What the heck are they?"

"No idea." I didn't know how to explain them, so I'd go with avoidance.

We sprinted up to the base of the tower, and he leapt onto it without stopping.

I stumbled to a halt, panting. "You have got to be kidding me. We can't just take the elevator and stairs?"

"They don't access the very top. You want the good stuff, you have to work for it." He looked behind him, searching for the hellhounds. "Come on, before the hellhounds wake up!"

Yeah, that was enough to encourage me. I leapt onto the tower, grabbing the iron with my hands. It wasn't an easy climb, but I scrambled after him, feeling my heart thud in my chest like a giant freaking drum. There was *no* way I could look down.

Up. Up. Up.

I put hand over hand, ignoring the cold fear that threatened to freeze my muscles and leave me clinging to the side of the tower like a freaking ninny.

Lachlan climbed like a pro, moving quickly and with such complete assurance that I was sure he scaled mountains daily.

I turned my attention back to the tower. The metal was slippery beneath my hands, but at least the rain wasn't falling on my face. Suddenly, I realized that Lachlan had been keeping me dry this entire time, even when we'd been separated and running across the field, pursued by the beasts of hell.

It was just enough to distract me from the fear, and I kept climbing. My muscles ached and my lungs burned as we went ever higher.

I glanced up. Still a third of the way to go.

Three pairs of eyes peered down at me.

The Cats of Catastrophe sat on a higher metal bar. They looked wet and miserable—Princess Snowflake III, particularly, with her wet white fur plastered against her body, making her look like a skinny rat. She hissed at me.

Hairless Muffin couldn't look any skinnier, and Bojangles looked even more insane than usual, his head tilted to look down on me and his fur mussed on his head. The expression on his face said I was an idiot to be climbing all the way up here. I couldn't help but agree.

But how the heck had *they* gotten up there?

I shook my head. Not important. Not when I needed all my strength and all my wits to survive this.

I continued to climb, my muscles aching and my hands freezing against the wet steel of the tower. Though my skin was chilled with fear, I never looked down. That way lay madness.

Up. Up. Up.

The cats watched.

Lachlan climbed silently beside me.

As we neared the top, the tower narrowed, forcing Lachlan and me more closely together. I could hear his breathing, even and calm. Far different from my breath, which heaved in and out of my lungs. Terror made me breathless, and every foot that I climbed seemed to reinforce the idea that *this. Was. Dumb.*

A girl afraid of heights climbing the Eiffel Tower?

Yeah, not great. My muscles trembled with strain and fear.

"Are you okay?" Lachlan asked from beside me.

"Fine." My response was short. I kept my gaze on the tower and continued to climb.

We were close. Not much farther now.

Which also meant that we were hundreds of feet above the ground. If I fell, that gave me a long time to think about the crash that was coming.

I reached for the next rung.

My hand slipped.

Then my foot.

A scream caught in my throat as I dangled, barely able to hold on with one hand.

Lachlan reached down, grabbing me. His strong hand gripped my wrist, cementing my hold. My heart thundered as I went into tunnel vision.

"Ana! I've got you!" Fear spiked Lachlan's voice.

I swallowed hard and focused, pulling myself back from the edge. Blood roared in my ears as I reached up with my dangling arm, scrabbling for purchase.

"I won't let you go." Lachlan's voice was my lifeline.

I looked up, meeting his gaze. It grounded me, calming the panic. Finally, my fingertips closed over the cold metal, and I gripped it hard. My foot found a metal bar, and I clung to the tower, panting.

"You can let go," I wheezed.

"Are you sure?"

I nodded, squeezing my eyes shut and focusing on the reassuring feeling of the cold steel beneath me. He had saved me—been my lifeline in that moment—but I had to rely on myself. On my grip on the steel and my own muscles to pull me out of this.

"We're nearly there," he said.

"I know." That was part of the problem. But I didn't focus on how far away the ground was.

Lachlan's grip released me, and we continued to climb. I felt for every metal rung on the tower-ladder, focusing harder than I ever had in my life.

By the time I finally scrambled onto the top, my heart was thundering and my skin felt like ice.

Princess Snowflake III stared at me, her gaze unimpressed.

My cheek pressed against the cold steel floor as I looked at her. She was *more* than unimpressed.

Stupid.

Yeah. I had to agree with her.

Bojangles ran up to me and licked my nose, his tongue rough as sandpaper and smelling of fish.

"I like you, too." I pushed myself up onto my hands and knees, trembling. Crap. I was so weak I'd never be able to walk again. Or at least, not for an hour.

Muffin walked up to me, then pressed his paw to my hand. Magic flowed through me, bringing strength and warmth with it.

I looked into the green eyes of the hairless cat who looked like he'd been in one fight too many. "What's that?"

"Meerow." *Magic, you moron.*

I smiled. "Thanks."

I scrambled to my feet, stronger now.

Lachlan stared at me, a curious expression on his face. "You're afraid of heights."

I shrugged.

"Why didn't you say so?"

"It wouldn't have made the fear go away."

He nodded, respect flashing in his eyes. "You're tough, Ana Blackwood."

"Highest compliment you could give me." In my world, toughness was what kept you alive.

"You also brought along some friends?" He pointed to the cats.

"New buddies." Though I had no way to explain the magic that had just flowed from Muffin.

"Do you know who they are?" he asked.

"Muffin, Princess Snowflake III, and Bojangles."

"The black one with no fur—is that Muffin?"

"Yes."

He turned his appraising gaze to me. He was clearly impressed. "He's the Cat Sìth. And he's chosen you."

"The what?"

"A mythological Scottish creature."

Uh. I turned to look at Muffin. "So you run a racket with your cat gang down in Edinburgh, *and* you're some fancy mythical cat?"

I'm a cat of many talents.

"What is the Cat Sìth exactly?" I asked.

"A bit like a fairy cat."

Muffin hissed. *I'm no fairy cat! I'm more like a dragon!*

Lachlan didn't appear to have heard Muffin, so I translated. "He didn't like that."

"My apologies, King of Cats."

Muffin inclined his head, accepting. It seemed he could be gracious when called a king.

"It appears he's bonded himself to you," Lachlan said. "The Cat Sìth doesn't choose just anyone."

I looked at Muffin. "Probably a mistake, right?"

Muffin shrugged, and it was good enough for me.

It was time to drop this discussion, so I spun in a circle, taking in the platform at the top. It was tiny, with no railing on any of the sides and a vertical spear of metal right in the middle. Like a small flagpole.

My head whirled. The city spread out around us, golden lights forming a rolling blanket over the earth. "This is amazing. I'm surprised it's not crawling with tourists."

"Humans can't see it. To them, it doesn't exist. They stop at the lower level and go no farther."

"Wow." I rubbed the back of my neck, trying to drive away the uncomfortable tinge. "And it's super hard to get to."

"True enough."

I glanced at him. He'd saved my life. "Thank you."

He nodded, then reached into his pocket and withdrew the crystal. He took a few steps to reach the post in the middle of the tower. "This is where most of the magic in Paris resides. It's like a beacon, drawing on the power in the city and magnifying it." He placed the crystal on top of the flagpole, sliding it onto a little spike.

I stared at it, waiting.

Nothing happened.

"What now?" I asked.

"It needs moonlight." He looked up, a frown on his face. "And the moon needs a little help."

He raised his hands, looking like an ancient warlock. Rain fell around him in a circle, never landing on him.

Princess Snowflake III went to join him, sitting at his side. Clearly, she liked him. It was dry where I was, but she had eyes only for Lachlan.

Magic flared on the air, the scent of pine and the taste of caramel. Light glowed around his hands, illuminating his handsome face and dark eyes.

The breath caught in my throat as his magic rolled over me, soaring toward the sky above.

I looked up, searching for the moon that was hidden behind clouds. A faint glowing patch caught my eye, and wonder filled me as the clouds moved away from the moon, revealing a bright white orb.

I'd seen a lot of powerful magic, but I'd never seen anyone move the clouds before.

The moon's light shined on the crystal, making it glow bright white. A beam of sharp light streamed forth from the glass, blinding me. I stepped left to avoid it, then turned, following the beam that was like a spotlight.

It shined over the city, landing on the ground in the middle of a huge intersection. Cars zipped through the light, but it was shining right in the middle of the ground.

"It's shining on the street. But there's nothing there," I said.

"Under the street." The moon's light disappeared, and I realized that Lachlan had let the clouds return to their natural position. "The sewers in Paris are famous."

"Sewers?" Just my luck. First heights, now...

I didn't want to think of it.

"Let's go, then." I shot Princess Snowflake III a look. She wouldn't like the sewers, but she was talented enough to keep her fur white, I'd bet. Bojangles, on the other hand, didn't look like he'd care either way. And Muffin was his usual stoic self.

"The climb down will be worse. Can you manage?"

"I can manage." But I sure wouldn't like it.

6

As Lachlan had said, the climb down was worse. I hadn't slipped, thank fates, but was still wobbly when I reached the bottom.

Muffin had stayed at my side the whole time. The little gremlin pressed his paw to my hand every time he thought I was faltering, and muttered helpful things like *Don't quit now, lily butt.* I had no idea what a "lily butt" was, but I'd be lying if I said it hadn't helped.

We hit the ground running—me on shaky legs and Lachlan on much sturdier ones. Fortunately, we didn't alert the hellhounds to our presence. Or maybe they were scared off by the sight of our feline guardians.

Lachlan had recognized the location of the intersection, so I followed him, racing along the rainy streets of Paris, past fashionable people with dark umbrellas and silk scarves that cost more than my yearly income back in Death Valley.

When we reached the intersection, I stared. "Crap."

"That is a lot of traffic."

"Understatement."

The cars whizzed by, headlights golden in the rain. As

expected, right in the middle of the intersection was a manhole leading to the sewers.

"I can buy us a minute," he said. "Exactly a minute, so follow everything I do."

I glanced at him. "What do you mean?"

But he was already holding up his hands, magic surging on the air. I loved the scent of it, so fresh in the middle of the city.

Then the air became thick, almost difficult to breathe. I sucked in a gasp, grateful when it slowly filled my lungs.

The cars in the street began to slow. The people around us, too. Finally, the cars stopped, yellow lights frozen in the gleaming rain.

"Holy fates. Telekinesis?" I asked. If so, it was the most powerful I'd ever seen. Moving one object was hard. But hundreds?

"Not quite. I can slow time around myself."

"Why don't you do this in a fight?"

"It wouldn't matter. I can't interfere with the objects that I'm controlling, or something terrible could happen. But come on. We don't have long." Sweat dotted his brow. Clearly, this took some serious effort.

He sprinted into the street, and I followed. The Cats of Catastrophe were close on my heels, though Bojangles kept getting distracted by the bright lights of the cars.

It was eerie, and scary. There were enough cars that we'd be pancakes if they started up again.

Lachlan bent and pulled off the heavy manhole cover. The Cats of Catastrophe dived in first, scraggly Muffin leading the way. Princess Snowflake III gave the hole a disdainful look, then leapt in with a shudder. Bojangles ran right in without hesitating or even looking. He was like the Road Runner going off a cliff.

I followed, climbing down the iron ladder into the gloom.

Lachlan came behind me, and as soon as he pulled the manhole cover back over the hole, the roar of traffic started up again.

"Too close," I muttered.

"Aye."

I hopped onto a stone sidewalk built along the side of the sewer, and I raised my hand to illuminate my lightstone ring. It flared golden, revealing the space all around us.

I turned, taking in the wide stone tunnel that stretched in either direction. Water traveled sluggishly at the bottom of the tunnel, smelly, but not the worst. I had a distinct feeling there were grosser parts of the sewer. Other tunnels jutted off this one, giving the feeling of a massive catacomb.

"There's a city under a city down here," Lachlan said. "The most famous sewers in the world."

"They should run tours."

"They do. But not of this part."

The Cats of Catastrophe were scouting out the ground ahead, sniffing all over as they inspected the walkway. The stone ledge that they walked on looked ancient, but at least it kept us out of the sewer water.

Something fizzled over my skin, a distinct feel of dark magic that prickled lightly. "You feel that?"

"Aye." He pointed to the right, to where the cats had gone. "Coming from that way."

"Let's go." I set off, following the sense of dark magic. *Where the heck are you, magic thieves?*

Something else pulled me along, too, though. A sense of my own magic, leading the way.

It spoke in my head, as if it knew the question I was asking and wanted to provide an answer.

What weird new power was this?

My Dragon God magic?

I shook away the thought. Now was not the time for distractions. We made our way through the tunnels, going deeper and deeper into the sewer. Water flowed sluggishly beneath, beginning to stink more strongly as we went.

The tunnel appeared to turn right as we neared, but I stopped, peering hard at the dead end in front of me.

Something in me tugged in that direction.

Did it *really* end here? It was an abrupt and strange way to divert a tunnel.

"Come on," Lachlan said. "We need to go right."

"Hang on." I held out a hand, reaching toward the wall that seemed to be a dead end.

"What the heck is past here?" I murmured, more to myself than to him.

It was something. I could feel it.

Look and you will find what you seek.

Magic seemed to fizzle in my mind. It was a guide, in my head. It hadn't worked before, but now it was?

It had a mind of its own.

The cats were sniffing at the base of the stone, clearly perplexed.

I stuck my hand out, ignoring the repellent sensation that the wall gave off. That was enough to convince me that there was magic here.

I pushed harder against the stone, and my hand disappeared through the wall.

"Bingo." I stepped through the false barrier, into a long stretch of tunnel on the other side.

Lachlan followed. "How did you know? Even your feline sidekicks didn't realize."

"Instinct." *Lie.* "Come on."

We hurried down the tunnel, toward the strong sense of dark magic that was ahead of us.

When flame burst to life ahead of us, my heart leapt into my throat. The wall of fire seared my skin, making my eyes water. I flung out my shield. The protective barrier burst forth, forming a semi-transparent white wall between us and the flame. The air cooled a bit, no longer hot enough to maim.

Panting, I inspected what was ahead. Nothing but fire.

Then my magic faltered.

My shield dropped.

Shit!

I stumbled backward, away from the flame that roared forth. Lachlan waved a hand, his magic flaring. Sewer water rushed from below, crashing against the flame.

It sizzled and died, smelling of hot garbage.

"Oh, thank fates," I muttered, leaning against the wall and gagging at the scent.

Panic followed quickly on relief's heels.

My magic had faltered again.

Change was definitely coming, and I couldn't let him know.

I caught his gaze, and it looked like he wanted to ask about my magic dying.

Fortunately, a massive splash sounded from behind him. My gaze darted to the water, where a huge serpent's head was bursting forth.

I drew my sword from the ether and lunged for the scaly black creature, slicing cleanly through its neck. Blood sprayed, but I was fast, dodging low to avoid it. It splattered the wall behind me.

I stood, looking at Lachlan. "You're welcome."

He nodded his thanks, then his eyes widened on something behind me.

Oh, shit.

Before I could turn, he pulled the same trick I had, yanking his two short swords from the ether and lunging. I spun in time to see him slice another sea creature across the throat.

It crashed back into the water, sparkly black scales shining in the light of my ring. Red eyes blazed with a demonic light, and the scent of dark magic surrounded it. Its blood flowed into the water, making it boil.

"They're magic," he said. "Not real."

"Guarding something." I stepped up to the edge of the platform and peered down, my heart hammering. "We'd better get a move on."

We hurried from the spot, keeping our gazes on the water beneath us. I glanced at Lachlan as we walked, taking in the controlled nature of his being.

He was like a tiger, always waiting to pounce. Ready for anything.

It was a warrior's stance. His stock and trade might be creating great magic to sell, but that wasn't all he was good at. If I couldn't have Bree or Rowan at my back in a fight, he was a good alternative.

As we walked, the air began to smell fouler. At first, I thought it might be the sewage. Were we coming to a particularly rank section?

But then my skin began to prickle.

"Dark magic," I whispered.

Lachlan nodded. "Close."

His magic swelled briefly on the air, the scent of pine cutting through the stink. I looked at him curiously.

"Blocking our sound, in case we're close."

"Ah." I remembered how Bree had said she couldn't hear us when she was eavesdropping. "You'd make a good thief."

"In another life, maybe."

Of course. This Lachlan was far too honorable for thievery. I was, too, now, though I hadn't always been. There were parts of my childhood—the parts after my mother's murder—where thievery had been the only way my sisters and I could eat.

I shook away the dark memories and focused on the sewer. We were entering an older part, where the brick looked more broken and the stone walkway more battered.

The dark magic was stronger here, and my heart began to pound.

We were close to something.

Up ahead, the passage branched off to the right.

Lachlan slowed as we neared, and I followed suit. The sound of voices filtered out from the passage on the right. There had to be a room there.

Up ahead, the sound of footsteps approached from another passage.

The Cats of Catastrophe, who'd been following along, hurtled off down the passage, hunting the owners of the footsteps. Lachlan and I pressed ourselves up against the wall, listening to the people in the room.

I crouched low, and he went high. We were crushed against the stone and against each other, but the sound of voices distracted me from the warmth of his body.

"When do we take it to her?"

"Soon. We have to wait for the signal. It's not safe to bring it until the sorcerer is ready."

"Not safe how? Sitting here with this thing is dangerous! People are after it!"

It? Were they talking about the spell that Lachlan had created? Were these our thieves?

Something in me screamed *yes!*

It might have been the new power that was trying to grow within me, or maybe it was common sense.

I looked up at Lachlan, whose big body loomed over me as he attempted to peer around the edge of the passage.

Well, if he was looking, I wanted to see, too.

I peeked around the edge of the stone passage, spotting a

room within. About twenty feet away, a group of demons and mages sat around a rickety table. A paper-wrapped package sat on the table between them.

Bingo.

I caught sight of silver circles tattooed on the backs of the necks that I could see. What was that all about?

"When will she want it?" one of the mages asked. He was a skinny guy with dark hair and mean eyes. "It's not safe here. For the spell, or for us."

"We're supposed to wait until she finds the sorcerer!"

I glanced up at Lachlan. How did he want to play this?

His gaze was glued on the group and the package, calculation in his eyes.

There were a lot of mages and demons in there—an even dozen—but we could take them if we had to.

"Oy! Who's there?" one of the voices shouted.

Panic flared as I looked back down at the group, just in time to see a massive fireball hurtle toward us. It glowed orange and fierce, and was easily the size of a small car.

I lunged away from the wall as it plowed into the corner. It hit the stone with such force that chips of rock flew off. One sliced across my cheek, and pain flared briefly.

It was forgotten as I scrambled to my feet. Lachlan hopped up beside me.

"Go!" He led the way, racing into the chamber and blocking the way so he'd take the brunt of any oncoming hit.

My heart thundered as I followed. This was our only chance. We'd alerted them, and they'd run. We had to get that package before they escaped.

As he raced for the group, magic swirled around him. It flashed bright, then a lion stood in his place. His fur and mane were pitch-black, a strange combination that was both beautiful and terrifying.

The beast that was Lachlan charged the demons. A demon threw a fireball, and I dived low, skidding on the ground as the hot flame passed overhead.

As I lunged to my feet, I drew my daggers from the ether.

The demons and mages were scrambling within, trying to mount their defense as Lachlan charged. He hit two of them at once, taking them to the ground.

I threw my daggers at two more, taking out a gray smoke demon and the fire demon who'd tried to turn me into a roast turkey. My steel blades sank into their throats, blood spraying.

As I called two more daggers from the ether, Lachlan rampaged through the room, taking out demons as fast as they could hurl their magic at him. He plowed through smoke bombs and dodged massive icicles, tearing limb from limb.

A shining blue icicle hurtled toward me, forcing me to dodge left to avoid the blow. It sailed so close to my cheek that I could feel the cold.

I ignored it, frantically searching the room for the package.

It was tucked under the arm of a skinny guy with blond hair and a rat's face. He was fumbling in his pocket, clearly searching for something.

A transportation charm!

It had to be. If he found it, he could disappear from here in seconds.

I threw my dagger at him. He seemed to sense it coming at the last minute and shifted. The blade sank into his shoulder.

He howled, panic flashing across his face.

I raised my other dagger, but pain tore through my shoulder, sending agony racing through my arm.

I looked down. A tiny dagger stuck out of my flesh.

I looked up, catching sight of a skinny little demon with pale skin and red horns.

"A taste of your own medicine," the demon hissed as he drew another blade from the satchel at his side.

I flung out my hand, creating a barrier between us and him.

The mage with the package was still fumbling in his many pockets, and Lachlan was working on the last six demons. He'd already mauled four of them.

The little white demon's blade bounced off my shield.

Pain sliced me through the middle, and my shield flickered.

I looked down, gasping.

There was no dagger protruding from my middle, though it sure felt like it.

My shield faded. Lachlan roared, a sound of obvious pain. Magic flared around him, and he shifted back to human.

Right in the middle of five demons.

His face was white and drawn. He looked like agony was tearing him apart. Just how I felt. Tears welled in my eyes as I struggled to stay upright. But he managed to draw his sword and turn toward the demons.

What the hell was going on? Panic made my heart race.

The little white demon hurled another blade. I was too weak and slow to stop it, and it sank into my thigh.

I ignored the demon who was hurling blades at me and looked to the mage with the package. I had one job here, and I had to finish it.

Shaking, I dragged a blade from the ether and hurled it at him, but weakness made my aim wonky.

The mage dodged the steel, pulling a little stone from his pocket.

"Lachlan!" I screamed. "Transport charm!"

But Lachlan was fighting for his life. His skill was still incredible—I'd never seen someone fight so well. Not even me and Bree, and that was saying something. But his speed was like that of a normal man's—not the crazy whirlwind I'd seen before. And he used no magic. Where the hell was his magic?

He was incredible with his blades, but he was far outnumbered by enormous demons. He needed his magic. They were overpowering him, delivering as many cuts as he gave to them.

My gaze darted to the mage with the package. He hurled a stone to the ground. Glittery black dust puffed up, and he stepped inside, disappearing.

I stumbled to my knees, pain taking me down.

The little white demon approached me, a grin on his face. The dagger gripped in his hand gleamed, but he didn't throw it. Clearly he wanted to make the kill up close.

"Bastard." I spit. Pain tore through my thigh and my shoulder where his other blades had hit.

I called a dagger from the ether, but came up short.

I was out.

Shit.

So I called on my sword.

On the other side of the room, the five demons abandoned their attack on Lachlan so they could race to the dissipating cloud of glittery black dust. They leapt through it, escaping the sewers before the transportation charm faded.

I staggered to my feet, facing the demon who approached.

I couldn't kill him—I needed to be able to question him.

He took one look at my blade, then my face. Indecision flickered over his ugly mug, and he hurled his knife. I dodged, barely, and the steel sliced over my arm.

"Bitch," he hissed, then ran.

He sprinted for the last of the black cloud. It was nearly gone. He might not make it. Too weak to chase, I threw my sword. It hurtled end over end and then plowed into his leg. He stumbled, giving it one last burst of speed, and made it through the glittery cloud, disappearing.

I stumbled to my knees.

Shit.

Triple shit.

"What happened?" I croaked.

Lachlan didn't answer. He was laid out on the ground on the other side of the room, surrounded by the disappearing bodies of the demons he'd felled.

I crawled to him, my wounds aching. Blood dripped down my arms and thigh, leaving a gruesome trail.

Lachlan was rising to sit, his face twisted in pain. Gashes covered his torso, the claws of some demon that had gone to town once he'd shifted back to his human form.

"Are you all right?" His gaze trailed over my body, concern replacing the usual blankness.

"Sorta?" I wasn't quite sure. The pain and blood loss were making me woozy. "You?"

"Same." Pain echoed in his voice, and frustration.

We'd lost the lead.

He dug into his pocket and withdrew a little vial. He uncorked it and took a tiny sip, leaving the vast majority of the potion in the bottle. Then he handed it to me. "Drink."

I didn't ask questions, just swilled the liquid. Warmth and comfort flowed through me immediately, relaxing my muscles and clearing my mind.

"What's in that stuff?" I asked.

"Healing potion. Enough for one."

"Thanks for sharing." My wounds weren't fully healed, but they were a bit better. Enough that I had the strength to stand.

So did he, staggering to his feet.

I stumbled toward the body of a disappearing demon. Its arms and legs were almost invisible now as the body returned to the underworld. I fell to my knees and dug through the creature's pockets. Demons didn't normally carry ID, but maybe I'd get lucky.

On the other side of the room, Lachlan did the same.

After a minute, there wasn't enough of the demon left to search.

"I've got nothing," I said.

"Aye, same here."

I staggered toward him. He wasn't looking much better.

"What the hell happened to us?" I asked.

"I don't know. Felt like my magic was being sucked out," he said.

"Can you make a portal?"

"I can try." He held out his hand. His magic barely flared.

Shit.

Slowly, a hazy portal appeared. Sweat dotted his brow, and his arm shook.

"Go!" he said.

I leapt through, letting the ether suck me in.

7

After a whirlwind ride, the ether spat me out in a field in the country. The moon shined brightly, and night bugs made a racket, chirping and screeching. I stumbled away from the portal exit, and Lachlan appeared, staggering.

"That was the last of my magic." His voice was strained, weak.

Fear turned my blood to ice. What was happening to us?

"Where are we?" I asked. We needed to be somewhere safe to figure this out.

"My country home." He pointed behind me, and I turned, spotting a pretty manor house that looked historic, though I couldn't pinpoint an age.

My feet felt like lead as I staggered toward it. Lachlan wrapped an arm around my waist, supporting me. Together, we stumbled toward the large stone barn in the backyard.

The heavy wooden door looked impossibly heavy as we neared. Lachlan pressed his right hand to a metal medallion set into the wood, and it glowed golden.

Magic sparked, and the door swung open. We stepped inside.

The scents of hundreds of magics bombarded me. Tables were cluttered with all manner of magical tools, herbs, and jars. He led me to one, his trembling hands seeking two large blue vials.

He handed one to me. "Drink."

I gripped the container in one hand, sinking to my knees near the wall. Apparently I'd lost more blood than I'd thought. I spun around to sit with my back against the wall. He joined me, and we quickly swilled our potions.

I rested my head against the stone wall as warmth and strength flowed through my body. Through bleary eyes, I stared at the ceiling above.

"It's a full dose." His voice sounded stronger. "You should feel better in a bit."

"You only travel with one potion?"

"I'm used to working alone."

"Maybe bring two from now on?"

He chuckled. "I will."

My vision began to clear as my body healed. Suddenly, I realized that I was leaning against his shoulder. His heat burned me, making my breath catch. I looked over at him, catching sight of him looking at me.

His dark eyes were warm as they traveled over my face.

My heart thundered.

Why did people call him cold? He wasn't that way. Not with me.

It almost looked as if he were leaning toward me, his eyes on my lips. Then reality seemed to hit him, and he looked away. The shutters closed over his eyes again. "We have a problem. Two problems."

"Our magic and the spell."

"Aye. Something happened back there. I had no control. My magic leached away like water pouring out of a tipped-over bucket. And when I made the portal to come here, it felt like I was using up the last of my power."

"My shield just faltered and died." Which actually wasn't that weird. My magic had been going haywire lately. But I'd felt the same pain he had, and it definitely felt like something was even more wrong inside of me. Though there was kind of an explanation for my magic faltering, there wasn't one for Lachlan. Or for the pain we'd felt.

That was the scary part.

Lachlan climbed to his feet.

"What are you doing?" I really didn't want to get up yet. Though my wounds no longer stung, every part of me ached. It felt like I'd run a marathon. No, two marathons.

"I'm going to test my magic. I won't go far. Stay here." His voice was unusually gentle. He looked away quickly, then went to the open door and stepped out. True to his word, he went no farther.

I watched his broad shoulders as he raised his hands. Nothing happened.

I sniffed the air, hoping for a hint of pine. Or maybe the taste of caramel on my tongue.

I smelled nothing. Tasted nothing.

Shit.

He'd tried to control the weather or move water or something and it hadn't worked.

He turned, his face dark. "Someone put a curse on us. I couldn't move the water in the nearby river."

"How do you know it's a curse?"

"It's the only thing that could do something like this." He shook his head as he sat down. "But I didn't see any of the mages use any magic that could do this."

"Not to mention, it's got to take a *lot* of power."

"An immense amount." He rubbed the bridge of his nose. "I

don't think our magic is actually gone. We'd feel a hell of a lot worse if they'd stolen it. But it's dampened somehow."

I tried to make a shield, but nothing happened. My magic was cold and dark inside me. I swallowed hard, fear rising.

I'd never felt this before.

But it was awful.

And it wasn't even as bad as it *could* be.

I had no idea if my missing magic was the result of this curse or a side effect of the Dragon God powers coming alive.

Probably both, with my luck.

"And we've lost all trace of the spell." His head thudded back against the wall. "Our only lead."

A small smile tugged at the corner of my lips. "Um, not exactly."

He turned his head, dark eyes suddenly interested. "Oh? Isn't your magic dead?"

"It is. But I have a clue." I called my dagger from the ether—the same one that I'd sent into the body of the mage who'd escaped with the spell. Fortunately, the ether storage spell was magic that didn't come from me. I'd bought it, so it still worked.

I held the blade up so Lachlan could see. The steel glinted dark red in the light. Dried blood coated the metal.

"I bought the cheaper storage spell, you see." I smiled. "Couldn't afford the one that cleaned my blades as well as kept them stored away."

"Just our luck." His appreciative gaze sent warmth through me. "A blood sorcerer should be able to track that blood. Give us a clue, at least."

"That's not one of your skills?"

"Sadly, no. But I know someone to call."

"Good." I did, too, but I couldn't afford their lofty prices. So I'd let him use his contact. My stomach grumbled loudly.

"First, let's get something to eat," he said. "We're running on empty right now."

"Good idea." I staggered upright. "I'm not sure how long I can keep going like this."

We left the workshop and cut across the lawn. I followed him toward the main house, struggling along a few steps behind.

He stopped and turned, then came to help me.

"I'm fine," I said.

"You're not." He hesitated just briefly, then looped an arm around my waist, seeming almost reluctant. I might've caught him giving me the occasional hot glance, but he wasn't keen on touching me, it seemed.

I was too weak to complain, though. I definitely needed the help.

By the time we walked through the wooden front door into the charming country manor, I could feel every inch of the blood coating me. It itched ferociously.

"Any chance I could get a shower before that meal? I can't stay like this." It'd give me some privacy to call my sisters, too.

He nodded, pointing left. "There's a bedroom through the living room. You'll find a bathroom there. I'll be in the kitchen."

"Thanks." I let go of him, staggering through the pretty foyer into the rustic French living room with a massive fireplace. The bedroom had the same decor—some kind of charming historic style that also conveniently looked like it could be in a catalogue.

The bathroom was large and sparkling clean, and the shower was spacious for an older home, with beautiful bronze fittings. I cleaned up as quickly as I could, leaning against the tiled wall for support.

I stepped out and dried off, relishing the feeling of being

clean before I realized that I'd have to put the same dirty clothes back on.

"Dang it." I bit my lip, debating, then headed out into the bedroom, determined to search for some clothes. There had to be something in here.

The old armoire revealed some dresses—short-sleeved casual ones dotted with flowers. The style looked like something out of the 1920s or maybe even older. Not my style, but I wasn't picky.

I reached for one.

"What do you think you're doing?"

The feminine voice made me jump. I nearly dropped the towel as I spun around.

A ghost stared at me. She was pretty, with long hair and an old-fashioned face. The kind that stared out of black and white photos inside frames that sat on lace doilies in grandmas' houses. She wore a similarly styled dress as the ones in the closet.

"I'm sorry," I said. "They're yours?"

"Who else would they belong to?"

"Um, someone alive?"

She harrumphed. "The living always get so much more respect than the dead! I'll tell you, I'm sick of it. It's one of the reasons I'm marching for voting rights, you know."

"Voting rights?" I eyed her old-timey outfit. "Like the suffragettes?"

"Exactly! I cut my teeth at the procession in 1913, but now I march for the rights of ghosts."

"Oh." My mind scrambled on an appropriate response. "Well done."

"Thank you." She inclined her head. "Now, who are you, and why are you rooting around in my closet?"

"I'm Ana. My clothes were destroyed, and I needed something clean. Do you mind if I borrow something?"

She extended a hand. "Go right ahead. But I'd choose a blue one. Better with your complexion. I'm Mildred, by the way."

"Okay. Thanks, Mildred." I pulled it off the hanger, but she didn't leave.

"You're here with the handsome man?"

"Lachlan? Yes."

Mildred sighed dreamily. "So good-looking. Very honorable, too, you know. He contributes to the local charity, and is very kind to the woman who takes care of the house. I think she's a bit batty, but he's kind to her anyway."

"You watch him?"

"What else is a ghost to do?"

"Move on?"

"And miss all the fun?" She scoffed. "I'm not going to waste my ghosthood like that!"

"So you like being a ghost?"

"Of course! I've wanted to be one since I was a little girl, so you can only imagine my delight when I perished young in a tragic hot air balloon accident."

Right.

"Of course. Only natural." This girl was nuts.

"I didn't want to take my own life, obviously. It's too precious for that. But I died early and by mistake, and now get to haunt the rest of eternity as a young, attractive ghost, so who am I to complain?"

"So you hang around here, mostly?"

"Sometimes. I make sure no one disturbs my bedroom. The attractive man has agreed to that, fortunately. And I do admit, I like to spend more time here now that he comes by occasionally."

"What can you tell me about him?" I was exhausted, had

dripping wet hair, and was standing nearly naked with a ghost, but I wasn't going to give up a golden opportunity for some dirt.

"That he's quiet. Keeps to himself. He makes dangerous magic and meets with dangerous people, but they respect him. Might even be a bit scared of him, actually." She shivered. "He's cold and tightly controlled. But he has to be. His power is immense and needs to be contained. I've never seen anything like it."

"What does he do in his free time?"

"Reads. Writes. Doesn't seem to have many friends. Just one guy. He comes by to help, but very rarely. He's a bit like an apprentice."

He had to be Decker, the friend who'd been abducted, if I had to guess. No wonder Lachlan was so intent on saving him. He was one of the loner's only friends.

"No family?"

"Not that I've seen." She shook her head. "Not even a photograph around the house."

That was really sad. My most prized possession—shared with Bree and Rowan—was a photo of our mother, who'd died when we were thirteen.

"I'll let you get dressed," Mildred said. "You look cold. And tired."

"I'm both."

"Good luck with the man. With whatever it is you are doing here."

"Thanks."

She smiled and drifted away, disappearing through the wall.

I returned to the bathroom where I'd discarded my clothes. I cringed as I stepped into my old underwear, then pulled on the dress that Mildred had recommended.

I turned to the mirror. "Wow."

I looked like Mildred. Like I'd stepped out of a time capsule. Not my usual style, but it was clean, so I'd take it.

I hurried out to the kitchen, which I found by scent alone. It was beautiful, looking just as I'd imagine a French country kitchen would look. Fresh flowers sat on the counter, no doubt courtesy of the kooky woman who managed the house.

Lachlan, his dark hair still wet from his shower, stood at the counter, cutting a block of cheese into slices. He looked up, then smiled when he caught sight of the dress.

It was the first smile he'd directed my way, and it was as devastatingly sexy as I'd imagined it would be. Heat coiled inside me, and I wanted to pat my cheeks to make it go away.

"I see that Mildred approves of you," he said.

"I think so. You have quite the roommate there."

He nodded. "I didn't realize I was getting a ghost when I bought the place, but I didn't have the heart to evict her."

"I think she spies on you."

"I think so, too. I try to ignore it." He picked up the tray of cheese and sliced meats. "I hope you like a cheese tray. Valerie, the housekeeper, dropped it off. Along with salad and bread."

"I'm always interested in cheese. Who isn't?" I sat at the table.

He set the tray down, then returned for the bread and salad. "Wine all right?"

I doubted he had any cheap champagne on hand, so I nodded. "Thanks. It'll probably put me to sleep."

"I doubt you need any help with that."

I put on a mock-offended voice. "What, do I look tired?"

"You look lovely, actually." Surprise flashed across his face, as if he couldn't believe he'd said that. Then all expression disappeared, and he sat across from me.

I blinked at him, trying to understand him.

I came up short, so I sipped the wine instead. He built

himself a sandwich that looked pretty manly. Lots of meat, some cheese, and two huge hunks of bread. I picked at mine, but quickly devoured at least two people's worth of cheese.

Once my hunger was sated, I looked at him. "Have you always been so powerful?"

He frowned. "No. But the potential was always there."

"How'd you develop it?"

"Practice." There was more story there, but he wasn't going to reveal it. Not now, at least. "How did you really end up at the Protectorate? Did they find you?"

"They did." I couldn't tell him the whole truth, but perhaps a part of it? "My mother died when we were young. Thirteen." Murdered by those who hunted us because we were Dragon Gods, but I wouldn't tell him that. "She had a feeling she would die young, so she wrote to them, telling them about us. That we'd need help."

"I'm so sorry." Concern flashed in his eyes, and his hand twitched. Almost as if he wanted to touch me in comfort.

Or maybe that was wishful thinking.

Truth was, I didn't think I'd turn down any kind of touching from him.

"It's fine." It wasn't. The pain was still sharp, but I didn't want to start crying. The Nile was my favorite river, and also my preferred way of coping. Denial could get one a long way.

"And the Protectorate came and got you?" he asked.

"No. They tried, because that's what they do—help people in terrible situations like ours." Though I wouldn't reveal quite *all* the details. Becoming orphans at thirteen was terrible enough. I doubted he'd pry. "But by the time they got to the homestead in Alaska where my mother had been raising us, we were gone. We had no way to survive there, so we left."

We'd also been running from those who hunted us, though

we hadn't known who they were at the time. We'd spent our childhoods running and hiding from an unknown threat.

"Then what?" he asked.

"Eventually, we made it to Death Valley Junction, the supernatural town in California."

"It's like the Old West, isn't it? I've heard of it."

"It's just like the Old West. Straight out of a John Wayne movie. We got odd jobs, and an older man helped us out some. Uncle Joe. Eventually, we got ourselves the buggy—an armored monster truck—and started doing runs across Death Valley, delivering outlaws to Hider's Haven."

He whistled low under his breath. "An armored monster truck that you call the buggy?"

"Yes. It's my one true love. Besides my sisters. And my painting."

"That's a lot of true loves."

"I have a lot of love to give."

He gave me an undecipherable look, as if he didn't know what to make of that, then said, "Driving across Death Valley is insanely dangerous."

"It is. But I'm brave. Good with weapons, too. We were the only ones willing to do the job. So you can see why the Protectorate wanted to hire us when they finally found us after all those years."

"I can. You're a woman of many talents."

The compliment warmed me, enough that I wanted to lean across the table and press my lips to his. But then, who was I kidding? I'd been wanting to do that for a while now.

I shoved back from the table, unwilling to make any kind of move. "Well, that's it for me. I need a few hours of rest, or I will fall over."

"I'll call the blood sorceresses in the morning," he said. "We'll get a lead on the mage who took the spell, then we'll go to the Protectorate and see if they have any answers about our missing magic."

I nodded. Damn, I hoped they had the answers we sought. Because we *really* needed them.

I woke up at dawn to the sight of Mildred sitting on the edge of my bed, staring hard at me.

I jumped, my heart thundering. "Holy fates, Mildred."

Happiness spread over her face. "Did I scare you?"

"Yep." I nodded. "Plenty. You're a fabulous ghost."

She stood, preening. "Thank you."

"No problem." I climbed out of bed, keeping the sheet wrapped around me. I'd had no nightclothes, and I hadn't wanted to borrow Mildred's. Wearing a ghost's clothes was really only something I wanted to do when absolutely necessary.

"You'd better hurry," Mildred said. "There are guests in the kitchen. Two women. A little scary."

"All right, thanks." I shuffled off to the bathroom, dragging my sheet like a tail. It didn't take long to get cleaned up and put on the dress again. My own clothes were so stiff from dried blood that they could have stood up on their own.

Mildred was gone by the time I made it out of the bedroom. The scent of coffee drew me towards the kitchen, along with voices.

When I reached the kitchen, I spotted two new faces. Familiar faces, actually.

A blonde woman and a black-haired woman sat at the kitchen table, both looking like they were dressed up for a night out on the town. The black-haired one wore a plunging black dress dotted with black crystals. The same gems ornamented her tall bouffant, and her eyes were coated in so much black makeup it looked like a mask. Her lips were blood red.

Mordaca, the blood sorceress from Magic's Bend. She was famous. And so was her sister, Aerdeca.

Aerdeca wore her signature white. But instead of the power suit I was used to seeing, she wore a white evening dress. Somehow, it was classy and scary, all at once. Her blonde hair slicked like water over her shoulders, and her blue eyes were cold.

"Ana." Mordaca's voice was raspy—the pack-a-day for forty years kind of raspy. Given that she couldn't be over thirty, it had to be natural. Her dark brows rose. "You're helping Lachlan."

I smiled as I went to the counter. "That I am. Thanks for coming to help with this."

They were the ones I would have called if I'd had to, but their prices made me cringe.

"He caught us just as we were heading out for the night." Aerdeca's voice was sweeter than Mordaca's, sounding like the trilling of birds. But it'd be stupid to assume she was any nicer or less dangerous.

"Late start, huh?" I said.

They lived in Magic's Bend, which was in Oregon. It had to be a good nine hours behind France. That would make it about 11 p.m. when they were headed out for the night.

"All the good parties start late," Mordaca said.

"So true." Aerdeca laughed, tapping her white nails on the surface of the table. "But it sounds like Lachlan needs our help more than Count Vladimir needs our attendance at his party."

"And he'll pay well for the privilege." Mordaca's dark eyes glinted with greed.

These ladies charged a fortune for their work, but they were worth it. Their shop, Apothecary's Jungle, was one of the most sought-after magic shops in the world. Hiring their services was sure to put a person into a lower tax bracket.

"So you think you can track the blood on the blade?" Lachlan asked.

"Of course, silly." Mordaca laughed. "And for you, we'll only charge half."

My gaze darted between them. Interest gleamed in Mordaca's eyes, which she couldn't keep from dragging over Lachlan. Since he was in the business of making dangerous spells, they should have been in competition.

But apparently Mordaca wouldn't let a little thing like work get in the way of her pursuit.

Aerdeca looked just as interested, in fact. I leaned against the counter and sipped my coffee, eyeing the plate of croissants on the other side of the room, licking my lips.

Mordaca stood. "Shall we get this show on the road? I'd like to make it to Vlad's before the meal starts."

"Of course." Lachlan stood, then led them from the room. I trailed behind, snagging a croissant off the kitchen counter as I went.

I bit into it as we crossed the lawn, then stopped dead in my tracks and stared at the croissant as buttery goodness exploded over my tongue. *Wow.*

So *that* was what a croissant was supposed to taste like. No wonder the world was obsessed. Too bad one had to come all the way to France to eat a decent one. I stuffed the rest of it in my mouth and vowed to go back for more.

Lachlan led the sisters to his workshop in the back. In the daylight, I could see the rolling vineyards all around. They were dormant now, the vines barren of leaves, but in the summer, it would be beautiful here. A river burbled by on the left. That was probably the water he'd been trying to control last night while testing his magic.

Lachlan, Mordaca, and Aerdeca stepped into the workshop. I

lingered outside for half a moment, calling on my magic, hoping to see if it still worked.

It sputtered inside of me, like a candle flame in the wind. I sucked in a deep breath and focused, trying to draw it to the surface as I held out my hand and envisioned a shield forming.

Come on. Come on.

I needed my magic. Without it, we didn't stand a chance.

A tiny flare of magic burst to life and exploded outward from my hand, creating a puny shield that wavered weakly.

I managed to hold it for a minute before it died.

That was weird.

So it wasn't fully gone.

I stocked the info away, hoping it would come in handy later, and joined the group in the workshop. Aerdeca and Mordaca were bustling around, going from table to table to gather supplies. Hundreds of varieties of herbs hung from the ceiling. I hadn't noticed them last night, but they smelled divine.

"That's the thing I like about working with you, Lachlan," Mordaca said. "We never have to bring our own materials."

I joined him at the side wall, pointing upward at the herbs. "Did you collect all of these?"

I had a hard time imagining him out in the fields picking flowers, then conducting the painstaking work of drying them.

"No. The housekeeper did. She knows what to look for." He smiled. "It's one of the main reasons I chose this place. Not only is it remote, it's also an excellent location for crafting dangerous spells, but the housekeeper is a brownie. She does all the work I don't want to do."

"And you focus on making the things that go bang."

"Essentially." He smiled. "A good system."

"Yeah. None of the boring parts."

"Exactly."

I turned my attention to Mordaca, watching as they dropped brightly colored potions into a stone bowl. The sisters hovered over it, one light and one dark, like two halves of a balanced whole. Their magic filled the air. Aerdeca's sounded like chirping birds and felt like a light breeze, while Mordaca's tasted of whiskey and smelled like cigar smoke. Together, they stirred it with a silver knife, then added droplets of their own blood. Last, they dipped my dagger into the mixture, melding some of the mage's blood with the solution.

The liquid smoked and burned.

My nose wrinkled.

From my position, I could only see Mordaca's face. Her brows rose as she stared at the smoke, which twisted and turned. I couldn't make out a pattern in it, but she clearly could.

"The blood bearer is in an ancient place, torn down by heat and the rage of nature. An ancient place of conquerors and villains that has grown again."

Wait—*what?*

"Could you clarify?" Lachlan asked.

Mordaca blinked, jerking her head back as if she were coming out of a trance. "There's an encryption on the bearer's blood. A concealment charm. That was all I was able to get."

"So the game continues." I looked at Lachlan. " Whoever stole from you is working hard to cover their tracks. The rest of the teams will need to stay on this, then. There are a hundred ways to interpret that."

Lachlan frowned. "At least a hundred." He turned his attention to Mordaca and Aerdeca. "Is there anything else you can tell us?"

"Only that whoever put the spell on this guy's blood is damned powerful," Mordaca said.

Yeah, I could have guessed that. But I kept my trap shut.

"I'd be afraid of them," Aerdeca said.

Oh shit. Aerdeca wasn't afraid of anyone.

Mordaca nodded. "I've never seen anything quite like this. It's intensely powerful and very dangerous."

Well, that wasn't good.

"Thank you," Lachlan said.

"You're welcome," Mordaca said. "We'll put it on your tab."

"Feel free to tip." Aerdeca grinned, and it was shark-like.

I winced. *That* was going to be expensive.

We said goodbye to them.

Once they'd disappeared, Lachlan looked at me. "We need to go to the Protectorate. Tell them everything has changed."

8

W e arrived at the Protectorate an hour later. Since Lachlan's magic was gone and he couldn't make a portal, we had to use one of his transport charms. They were rare and expensive, but this was kind of an emergency.

Unfortunately, because of Protectorate security, we couldn't transport directly within the walls. We chose the front gate, instead. The wind whipped across the mountains behind us, cutting through my leather jacket and thin dress. As I walked, my boots crunched down on icy layers of snow.

I clutched my bloody clothes in a plastic bag as I walked to the enormous wooden gate and pressed my hand to it. Magic flared briefly—the castle's magic, not mine, fortunately, since that was mostly gone—and the gate creaked open.

I gave the surrounding mountains one last glance—the Highlands really were the most beautiful place I'd ever been—then stepped through the gate.

Lachlan followed, and we made our way quickly toward the castle.

"Most of the staff will be gone," I said. "Off hunting the clue."

"Hopefully they'll be close enough to portals to return quickly," he said.

As we neared the courtyard in front of the castle, I saw more people than I expected. Lavender and Angus—two of the other students—along with our friends Caro, Ali, and Haris.

Caro looked at me from across the courtyard, her face pale. Ali and Haris didn't look any better, their dark complexions several shades lighter than normal.

I frowned. "Something is wrong."

"Do you feel that?" Lachlan nodded toward the castle door.

I turned my focus toward it. Magic rolled out from the castle, strong and fierce. It brought with it the sense of raw power, pushing and pulling against me like massive waves. I'd only felt it a few times before.

I gasped. "Arach!"

"The dragon spirit who started the Protectorate?"

"The same." I picked up the pace. Something was really wrong if she was making an appearance.

I hurried toward the entry. The massive wooden doors swung open, and I raced through into the hall. The feel of Arach's magic pulled me toward her office.

"This way." I led Lachlan through the corridors until we reached the room where Arach most often appeared. The few times I'd been in here, I'd loved this room. The walls were at least thirty feet high, and each was covered in brilliantly colored paintings. A fireplace always flickered warmly in the hearth. I could spend days in there.

I stepped inside, my eyes going straight for Arach. She was unlike any woman I had ever seen—primarily because she wasn't a woman at all. She was the spirit of a dragon in human form. Sort of human form.

She stood near the large fireplace, glowing with a pale white light. Her features were almost reptilian, and when she moved, she shimmered. As if she were only partially there. A ghost.

Long ago, when she'd been a flesh-and-blood dragon, she'd given her magic to help create this castle, and now she presided over it, guarding every generation of warriors and investigators and protectors who worked here. The Protectorate had been formed before the supernatural governments, a gift from the dragons meant to protect the other supernaturals who needed someone to fight on their side.

I loved their purpose and wanted so badly to be a part of it. To earn Arach's respect and a place here. She appeared rarely, though. Only when the situation was truly dire.

This was truly dire.

"Finally, you've arrived." Arach's voice rang with power. Her gaze moved toward Lachlan, who stood at my side. "You've been creating dangerous magic again, I hear."

"The world needs it, occasionally."

She nodded, reluctantly agreeing. "I suppose if it has to be made, then you should be the one to do it."

I shot Lachlan a surprised and impressed glance. Arach *respected* him.

Wowzers.

We had so much to tell her that I wondered where to start. But if she was here already, that meant the problem was probably worse than we realized.

"What's going on?" I asked. "You only appear when things are totally up a creek."

Her brows rose. "I assume you mean that we face a difficult challenge."

"It's as bad as we thought." A feminine voice sounded from behind me, and I turned.

Jude, the leader of the PITs, and Hedy walked into the room, their expressions tight and their eyes worried. The lavender-haired Hedy was the resident witch and inventor and one of my favorite people here. She was in charge of research and development, which often resulted in some very cool magic. Her silver dress gleamed like water as she crossed the room toward us.

"What is going on?" Lachlan asked.

"All of the individuals competing to find your missing spell have lost control of their magic."

I gasped.

"Including you, Lachlan," Arach said. "I can see in your aura that it is repressed."

"It is. But *everyone's* is gone?"

"Almost." Arach's eyes darted briefly to me, but she said nothing.

Was I the *almost*? I'd gotten my magic to work briefly this morning. Lachlan's hadn't worked at all.

"It has to be connected to the *ancientus* spell," I said. "Whoever stole it is worried that we're getting close. He—or she—is trying to stop us."

"I think that's likely," Jude said.

"They've repressed your magic, though," Hedy said. "Not stolen it entirely. So there is still hope. But we must work quickly to save everyone."

"Whoever stole the spell has evil plans for it," Arach said. "They must want to bring back some kind of dark magic from the past. We cannot let them."

The only way to do that was to recover the spell.

Fates, there was no turning back now.

Not that I'd ever planned to, but we were in serious trouble, and the only way out was forward.

If I had a tiny bit of my magic left, maybe my new seer ability could be used to find it. I needed to try, at least.

Everyone was talking now, debating theories and options. I slipped away, moving silently out the door and into the hall.

I was only a few steps from the room when Bree and Rowan hurried forward. Their gazes brightened when they saw me.

"You're back!" Bree said. "Dressed weird, though."

I looked down at the floral dress I was still wearing. "Borrowed it from a ghost. Did you just return?"

"Just now," Rowan said.

"How's your magic? Do you still have it?"

They both shook their heads.

"Mine's gone," Bree said.

"Mine's same as ever." Rowan grimaced. "Gone."

I gave her a sympathetic look.

"How are you?" Bree asked.

"I don't know." I frowned. "I may not have lost my magic totally, but I have no control over it."

"The transition?"

"I think so. My premonition power worked a bit when we were in the Paris sewers. It just showed up, guiding me. Never came when I called, though. But my shield is wonky."

"Did you find anything in Paris? We struck out in London. Thought we were onto something, but it was a bust. Then our magic disappeared."

"We almost had it," I said. "But the thieves got away."

"We should ask the FireSouls," Bree said. "This is more difficult than I expected, but they could find it."

"Apparently Jude already asked," I said. "They're busy with some emergency."

"Damn." Bree frowned. "That means two things are seriously wrong in the world right now."

"Exactly," I said. "But I want to head to the library to try to interpret the newest clue that we got. Maybe I can jog my premonition power. Want to come with—"

"Ana." Arach's powerful voice sounded from behind me.

I turned.

She drifted gracefully toward me, not so much walking as gliding.

"Arach. Did Lachlan fill you in?"

"Yes, he did. It sounds like you did well in Paris."

"We failed."

"But you got another clue." Her gaze assessed me, seeming to pry into my soul. "All of the competitors will be given the new information, and the hunt will begin again."

"New information?" Bree asked.

"It will all be explained at the meeting in the round room in thirty minutes." She turned to me. "But you, Ana. Something is different about you."

"Um." I swallowed hard, hesitating briefly. It was still hard to just blurt it out after so many years of hiding. But my secret was safe with her. I sucked in a deep breath and spit it out. "I may be transitioning to Dragon God. But I have no control over my power. I'm a mess."

She nodded. "I can see it in you. But your magic has not been fully repressed like everyone else's. There's still a light within you."

"A light? Is that how my magic has always looked?"

"No. When you first came here, you looked like any other supernatural. You had your magical signature, but no light from within."

"Do you think it could be my new gift of premonition?"

"Maybe." Doubt flashed across her face. "But I'm not sure. I wouldn't imagine it would manifest that way."

"Do you know which pantheon my magic might be from?"

She shook her head. "Premonition, or this light power, could be from any of them."

The light power had only made an appearance once before, more than a month ago, back when I'd been helping Bree and the sickness wraiths had attacked.

"I think the light is protecting you," she said. "It looks like a healing light of some sort. It's protecting you from the curse that is attacking everyone else."

"You're the only one left with magic," Bree said. "Out of all of us."

"You're special, Ana," Arach said. "I think the success of this mission may come down to you. Give it everything you have. Whatever magic is inside you—*use it.* Use your premonition gift to find the spell. The Protectorate needs you."

"But I have no control over it."

"You must obtain the control. You need to save yourself, but also everyone else. Save your friends. Save your sisters."

Fates. No pressure.

I swallowed hard and nodded.

"Good. I'm counting on you." She spun on her heel and drifted away, back into her room.

I turned to my sisters, knowing that my face was probably white as a sheet. "I need a Plan B. There's no way I can just call on my premonition power and solve this."

"Any idea what it will be?" Bree asked.

"Well—"

Two other students stepped into the hall. Lavender and Angus. The jerks. They eyed me as they passed.

"She doesn't stand a chance," Lavender muttered, just loud enough for me to hear. "Not qualified to be here."

I seethed but shoved the anger down deep. I didn't have time to respond. Not when so much was on the line. "I'm going to the library."

"What about the meeting in the round room?" Rowan asked.

"Skipping. I really need to get started on this, and I need something to help jumpstart my premonition sense, since I certainly can't do it on my own. Will you update me if anything happens?" I tapped the comms charm around my neck.

"Sure," Bree said. "We'll tag team this."

"Good luck in the library with Potts." Rowan shuddered.

The day librarian was a mean old bastard. Given the choice, I'd have waited until night, when Florian, the ghost librarian, took over.

But time was the last thing I had.

"Thanks, guys." I left, hurrying down the hall toward the library. I passed more than a dozen people on my way, and every one of them looked dejected and stressed.

They were all hunting the spell, and they'd lost control of their magic. I almost thought I could see the dark shadow of magic that surrounded them, repressing their power.

I was nearly to the library when Caro, Ali, and Haris turned the corner and bumped into me.

Caro's platinum hair gleamed, but her eyes were duller than normal. Her silver leather jacket was speckled with blood—not her own, from the looks of the pattern.

Ali and Haris weren't kicking their usual hacky sack between them, and their dark skin was pale. Their eyes were also duller.

"How's your magic?" I asked, even though I knew.

"Gone." Caro frowned.

"It's the bloody worst," Ali said.

"Second that," Haris added.

"Where are you going?" Caro asked. "There's a meeting in the round room."

"Library." I explained my plan.

Caro grinned, the first sign of the spunky girl I was used to. "I like how you think. But we've got some info that might help."

"Italy," Ali said.

"Italy?"

"Exactly." Caro nodded. "We were in Beijing, tracking word of new bad guys in town. We came across a group with a silver circle tattooed on the back of their necks."

My eyes widened. "So did I. In Paris."

Ali's gaze sharpened. "It must be their symbol."

"And maybe Paris wasn't the only invader's city that these guys were in," I said.

"It sounds like a large operation," Haris said.

"No kidding." Caro gripped my shoulder as if to impress upon me the seriousness of the situation. "This group—the ones in Beijing—they mentioned something about a drop-off in Italy."

"Dropping off the spell, maybe." My heart thundered. "This is a good clue."

"So Italy means something to you?" Ali asked.

"It could. I have an idea where to look. A rough clue. Lachlan will tell you all about it in the meeting. I have a feeling the teams will split up again, each going after different info."

Haris rubbed his hands together. "The race continues."

Caro grinned. "I like it."

"Good luck," I said. "Let me know if you learn anything else."

"Will do." Caro grinned and turned, then looked back. "When this is all over, you've got to teach me how to paint, okay?"

I nodded. I'd promised her earlier, but we hadn't had a chance. Not that I knew what to teach her. I just painted by instinct, slopping colors on in whatever order appealed to me. Fortunately for me, it usually looked damned good.

But I liked the idea of having a friend date. I wouldn't trade my sisters for all the gold and kittens in the world, but it was nice to have another friend. We'd lived on our own so long, wary and afraid of forming connections.

I turned and headed toward the library. The heavy wooden doors beckoned, and I pulled them open. As soon as I stepped into the massive, book-filled room, the fireplaces on each wall burst to life. The orange flames shed a warm glow on the brightly colored leather spines of the thousands of books in the library. Paintings hung on the walls—some of them even hung over the books, and they all glowed in the light of the fire.

High against the wall, I caught sight of Mayhem, the winged ghost pug. She had a rag gripped in her teeth and was rubbing it against the spines of the books.

"Earning your keep?" I asked her.

She yipped.

In front of the fire, two plush dog beds contained the other Pugs of Destruction—Chaos and Ruckus. They snored in front of the flames. Chaos's devil horns glinted in the light, while Ruckus's fangs gleamed on either side of his lolling tongue.

I grinned at them, then searched the library for any sign of Potts, the day librarian. He'd chew my head off if I messed around in his library without him knowing it. I was willing to face down a half dozen demons, but I was *not* willing to get on Potts's bad side more than I already was.

"Oooooh, ooooh!" Ghostly wails echoed from somewhere in the library's recesses.

I grinned.

Jackpot. It was Florian, my favorite ghost librarian. Bonus— I'd get to avoid the miserable Potts too.

"Oh my fates, what terrifying apparition is this?" I cried, laying on an accent that I most closely associated with a rich lady from the 1800s.

It probably sucked.

A ghost drifted out from the wall. He was young, with thick glasses that magnified his eyes and clothes from the eighteenth century. His fancy wig was a bit askew, but I wouldn't dare tell him. Florian Bumbledomber, the ghostly night librarian, could be quite sensitive.

"Did I scare you?" he asked.

I nodded. "Totally."

It was Florian's greatest hobby, scaring the library visitors.

"I'm glad you're here, but why isn't Potts? It's the middle of the day."

"He had to attend the meeting in the round room." Florian sniffed, as if offended he hadn't been invited. "So I've taken over for him."

"Thank fates," I said. "Because I really need your help."

He brightened. "You do? But why aren't you at the meeting?"

"I'm hunting answers. I already know what they'll talk about." I tapped my comms charm. "And Bree will update me."

"Excellent plan. What do you need?"

I explained the clues I'd been given—an ancient conqueror's city, likely in Italy. A place that was literally *full* of ancient cities.

"Ooh, that's a doozy," he said. "There are quite a lot of places like that there. You're going to need the ghost library."

I smiled. I loved the ghost library.

He led me toward the far wall, which towered high, piled with books, then veered toward the left corner. A large wooden door was hidden in a nook, and he pushed it open.

A wall of cold air rushed out, carrying along the scent of paper and leather and magic. Shining sparks drifted on the air as I followed him into the best part of the library.

It was an enormous circular area, making the huge room we'd left behind look miniscule. We stepped out onto a platform in the middle of the ten-story space. The walls soared high above us and dropped down far below. The huge empty section in the middle allowed me to see all of the circular levels filled with books.

Florian drifted onto the platform, sighing with contentment. "My domain."

It was much grayer and darker than the other library—but it was *massive.* And there was something hauntingly magical about it.

Beams of light streamed down from the domed ceiling above, and dust motes glittered in the air. Shining golden balls of light floated near the ceiling.

There were hundreds of nooks and crannies and different sections, all crammed with millions of books. I'd been here a couple times before, and it was still a maze my mind could hardly comprehend.

I walked toward the railing, realizing that no stairs had appeared to admit me to the rest of the library like they often did. Which meant there was no way to access the books. If I jumped over the railing, I'd plummet five stories to the huge mosaic map that made up the floor.

No thanks.

I turned to Florian. "Do I have to make a contribution?"

He looked around. "It seems that the library demands it."

Dang. I chewed on my lip.

In order to access this part of the library, one had to occasionally make an offering. The first time I'd been here, Bree and I had been in search of answers. In order to gain access and get those answers, we'd written down everything we knew about crossing Death Valley.

The library had been pleased and traded us info for info.

But this time? I'd already told the library all the good stuff I knew.

What new thing could I contribute?

Florian took his usual seat by the door to wait, and I walked toward the table at the side of the platform. It was piled high with empty books and magical pens. All I had to do was think of something that I alone knew, and then put magical pen to magical paper.

And voila!

Except....

I was fresh out of original ideas. I fiddled with a pen as my gaze traced over the table, catching sight of a box. It was ornately carved and about as large as a takeout pizza.

Muffin sat on top of the box, staring at me.

"Where'd you come from?"

Just being helpful.

Mayhem, the winged pug, flew into the room. She made a beeline for Muffin but didn't chase him. The Cat Sìth was much scarier than Mayhem anyway. Muffin jumped off the table to join Mayhem.

Off to find some hams. He flicked his tail. *Use your talents.*

Use my talents? I watched him trot away, then opened the box. An array of paints and brushes sat there.

Was that new? I hadn't seen this last time I'd been here.

A flash of white near the corner of the desk caught my eye. I leaned over and looked. Canvasses.

Clearly the library wanted me to paint it something. I had no idea what, but since I didn't feel prepared to write a treatise on something, I picked up the canvas.

This, at least, I understood.

I propped it on the desk, picked up some paints, and squirted colors on the palette that had sat under the paint box. I chose red on instinct, putting a broad swath across the white canvas.

Most of my painting was done this way, colors flowing out of me like words. I rarely had a plan—just followed what was in my soul. Ever since I'd been little, painting had fascinated me. You could *make* your own reality on the canvas. In a world that had been full of fear and hiding, that had been intoxicating.

But we'd never had the money for supplies, or the time. I'd put my creativity into the buggy, which had provided our desperately needed living.

As a result, the buggy was an incredible work of art, though some might mistake it for simple machinery.

But it wasn't painting.

Something in this spoke to my soul in a different way.

So I kept at it, imagining what the library might want. As I worked, magic began to flow through me. It started as a tingle in my stomach, then spread out to my limbs. Unmistakable, but also a bit foreign.

It was the new magic.

The prophecy or seeing or sight or whatever it was.

The magic directed my hand, taking over instinct and melding the two together. I chose brown, slashing it on the canvass. Then a lighter beige, black, white. The painting that began to form was unlike anything I'd ever painted.

I covered up the slashes of bright color, replacing them instead with a more realistic rendering of a trapdoor in the corner of the library. It was beaten and old, with the corner of a bright rug overtop of it.

When I stepped back, finished, the strangest sensation came over me.

That door was real. And it was somewhere in the library.

"Finished?" Florian asked, his voice sleepy.

I turned. As usual, he'd fallen asleep in his chair while waiting.

He stood and came closer. His eyes widened. "What is this?"

"I have no idea." I set the paintbrush down. "I painted it, but magic directed my hand." I could probably tell Florian about the prophecy power I was beginning to develop—we could trust the ghost.

But old habits died hard.

He leaned toward the painting and squinted. "That's the southwest corner of the ghost library. Rarely used anymore. I didn't realize there was a trapdoor under there."

"Did I find it?"

"I suppose we'd have to check to see if it's really there." He stood upright, then pointed to the railing that separated the plat-form from the rest of the library.

Magic swirled around it, and the railing disappeared, replaced with stairs leading down to the next level. "The library seems to agree that you've contributed something of value, though."

"Can we go check out that trapdoor? Like, now?" I needed to know. Had my power really found something that even Florian didn't know existed?

9

"Let's go!" Florian's voice was tinged with excitement, and he rubbed his hands together. "An adventure! To find a secret passage."

I grinned and followed him down the stairs, around the lower level to the left. Occasionally, the ghostly form of Mayhem, the winged pug, appeared in the corner of my vision. She must already be done with the hams.

"How are you able to say which part of this round room is the southwest corner? It has no corners."

"I guess, mostly." He grinned. "It's my domain. I do what I want."

Fair enough. He led me toward a set of bookshelves that looked just like the ones I'd painted. And there the rug, though it was no longer as bright as it had once been. As I'd painted it in my picture.

So had my power seen into the past as well?

Weird.

Florian bent down and flipped up the rug.

It revealed only bare wooden floor.

Shit.

But relief followed. Was this good or bad, that my magic hadn't been a real vision?

Did that mean I was going insane?

Florian frowned. "This can't be right."

"No?"

He knelt down and began knocking at the wooden floorboards, inspecting the edges of each piece of wood. As he worked, he hummed to himself.

I got down on my knees, joining him. As I poked at the floorboards, I wasn't sure if I wanted to find something or not.

Then my fingertips slipped into a larger than normal crevice between the boards. The board jiggled. I pulled it up easily.

"Florian."

He swung around from where he was kneeling, eyes brightening. "Now *this* is something!"

We removed the board, which made it easy to pry up the next one and the next. Soon, we'd revealed a trapdoor, long ago covered over by a false floor.

"Wow." I looked up at Florian. "That's cool."

"Indeed." He pulled on the trap-door, but it was locked. He yanked harder, straining. His wig tipped to the side, going slightly askew.

Mayhem appeared, little wings fluttering wildly to keep her chubby body aloft, and she pulled at the back of his coat, trying to help. Then Muffin appeared, joining the endeavor with Mayhem.

I stifled a laugh. Their efforts weren't doing much, so laughing out loud would just add salt to the wound.

"Let me try." Some ghosts could interact with the real world, but they weren't always very strong. I replaced Florian, pulling on the metal ring on the trapdoor. Magic sparked against my hands, and the door held fast. "It's enchanted."

Florian grinned. "That means there is something good down there!"

I wondered if it had anything to do with the mystery I was trying to solve but doubted it. I'd painted the door, revealing it as my admittance price to the library, but I felt no pull toward it. Whatever was down there interested me, but I didn't think it held answers to my most pressing problems.

So unfortunately, it would have to wait.

"I'll come back to help with it later," I said. "But right now, I really need to figure out where the thieves took the *ancientus* spell."

Florian nodded eagerly. "Indeed. That is a problem of the utmost importance." He shook his head. "What's happening to the people who are hunting it is terrible! To lose your magic." He shuddered. "Unimaginable!"

"Agreed." My magic was only partially gone, and it felt awful. I stood, turning to the library. "I'm trying to identify an ancient place, one torn down by heat and the rage of nature. An ancient place of conquerors and villains that has grown again." Mordaca's words came to me naturally. "And I think it's in Italy."

Caro's clue.

The magic in my comms charm crackled, and I touched the metal with my fingertips.

"Ana?" Bree's voice whispered out. "Another team found a clue. The name Abbondanza. No one knows who that is, though."

"Thank you, Bree," I said.

"One more thing," she said. "Another team found a group of demons wearing the silver circle tattoo. That makes at least five us to find them. We think that there are bases of operation all over the world."

And we were all working together to find the answer.

Competing to find the spell and win the prize, but together, we were finding the clues to solve this.

I smiled. This was my kind of place.

It fueled my determination to find the answer.

"Good luck," Bree whispered.

"That name sounds Roman," Florian said.

"It does, doesn't it? But Rome…" I felt nothing when I thought of Rome. Even though it was *the* conqueror's city, was it the one I sought?

Florian cleared his throat. "Dearest library. Could you help our guest?"

Nothing happened at first. Then a light glowed across the great open space in the middle of the room. It was two levels down, close to the bottom.

"Let's go!" Florian hurried off, a skip in his step.

I followed, my heart thundering as we neared the glowing light. A sense of excitement filled me. Of *knowing*.

There would be answers here.

We found a collection of dusty old books that were just begging for Mayhem's dusting cloth. In fact, she zipped forward, the rag gripped in her teeth, and shined up the spines of the books. Muffin had disappeared, no doubt to take a nap or steal something tiny.

I knelt down to inspect the books, but the golden titles were long faded with time. Gently, I pulled two off the shelf and stood. I turned, looking for a table and chairs.

The items in question were floating toward me, carried by a sparkle of golden magic. They stopped in front of me.

"I think the library knows you're doing important work," Florian said.

"Wow." Talk about cool.

I sat, slowly flipping open the pages of the books. The first showed the ruins of an ancient city. Herculaneum, in southern Italy.

It was from the Roman period. But I felt nothing.

I flipped through the next book, having no more luck. I reached for another, realizing the Florian was stacking them up next to me. "Thank you."

"For the cause."

I hoped I was up to the cause. My eyes began to cross as I carefully turned pages, looking at old illustrations and photographs of ancient sites all over Italy.

The problem was that our clues were so vague. The jerks who'd stolen the spell were probably laughing their asses off, knowing that they were so well concealed we'd never find them.

I couldn't blame them, though. After I'd seen Lachlan fight, covering my tracks like a super pro was the only way I'd ever steal anything from him.

I was on the last book when a page glowed with light. I blinked. "Florian, do you see that?"

"See what?"

Magic vibrated inside me, drawing me to the glowing page.

But the page wasn't glowing. It was my vision.

What the heck was this new magic?

It wasn't quite like being a seer.

But it was definitely guiding me.

"Pompeii?" Florian asked.

I looked at the image of the destroyed city. Bodies cased in ash lay in the street, a horrifying image of what had happened in the ancient town in 79 A.D.

"I guess so." I pointed to the word Abbondanza on the page. Apparently, it was a street in the destroyed city. "It looks like I'm going to Pompeii."

～

I made it back to the round room just as the meeting was dispersing. Bree and Rowan were already gone, but Lachlan stood near the front.

I pushed through the departing crowd and made my way up to him.

"Where were you?" he asked.

"Hunting answers. My sisters kept me informed during the meeting." I pointed to the comms charm around my neck.

"So that's why they were whispering. Did you find anything?"

"A couple of things." I thought of the trapdoor but didn't mention it. "I think the spell has gone to Pompeii."

"That's possible. It fits the clues. But why there?"

"Like you said, it fits the clues. And my gut is telling me." My gut being some unfamiliar new magic.

"Your gut told you Paris, too."

"It's a reliable gut." Okay, this convo was getting weird. "Should we tell everyone to look in Pompeii?"

I wanted that half-a-million-pound prize, but I wasn't going to risk the world to get it. We needed every advantage we could get.

"I don't think so," he said. "When the groups split up last time, they still found good information. And if your gut is wrong, we need more people hunting in other places."

He was right. There was no guarantee that my gut would be right—or that we'd find exactly what we sought in Pompeii.

"Okay, good. What about everyone's missing magic?"

"We think it's linked to the stolen *ancientus* spell. When we find the spell, we'll find the person who cursed us. But the Protectorate is trying to locate another solution in the meantime."

"Good. I don't like our chances of retrieving the spell without our magic."

"Agreed."

"I need to change before we go to Pompeii. Can I meet you at the entrance hall in thirty?"

"I look forward to it."

I hurried out of the room and raced up the stairs to my apartment door. I slipped inside and ran up more stairs—sometimes it seemed as if the castle was nothing but halls and stairs —and I slipped through into my apartment.

The Cats of Catastrophe were in my apartment again. Princess Snowflake III sat on the couch on top of two pillows this time, and she glared at me, as expected. Bojangles hung from the curtains. And Muffin was warming his butt on a pizza box.

"How did you get pizza?" I asked.

"Meow." *I'm freaking magical, dummy.*

"Got a slice left?" It was my favorite.

He meowed in what was clearly a laugh. I scowled at him, then hurried upstairs to change clothes. As I passed the easel set up along the side wall, I smiled. It looked like my panting had come in handy after all.

It didn't take long to change into fresh jeans, boots, and jacket. I took a moment to clean the blood off my blades. Even though I didn't have to see them while they were stored in the ether, I still knew they were filthy. I wasn't a neat freak by any means, but it still grossed me out.

I stopped by the kitchen on my way out, only to find that the cats had eaten all my food before they'd ordered the pizza. And this was after Muffin had presumably had some ham with Mayhem. Even a bottle of cheap champagne was open and empty.

I glared at Muffin.

He glared back. *Is this how you treat your guests?*

I sighed. "Just try to clean up after yourself, okay?"

There was no point in sticking around to hear his response. He was a cat. He was going to do whatever the heck he wanted.

Lachlan was waiting for me down in the main entry hall, but my stomach was still grumbling. "You hungry?"

"I could eat."

"Good. Let's grab something from the kitchen real quick." I led him down the stairs into the kitchen, the domain of Hans, the chef.

Hans's mustache quivered with delight when he saw us. He loved guests.

"Food!" he cried. "You must eat!"

"Could we do something quick to go, please? Something that won't put you out."

"But it never puts me out, *ma cherie!*" He darted about the kitchen like a ballet dancer, quick and determined. A little brown rat sat on the counter, a platter of cheese in front of him.

"How are you doing, Boris?" I asked.

The rat nodded, looking happy. Bree had rescued him from a crazy healer about a month ago, and now he spent his days either in the kitchen, mooching off of Hans, who was only too happy to oblige, or hanging out with Hedy while she created the spells and potions that we used so often.

Hans piled us high with sandwiches wrapped in paper, then he shoved a six-pack of juice boxes at Lachlan. "You must drink your juice!"

For whatever reason, Hans was utterly obsessed with giving people juice. It was the strangest thing, but he clearly felt strongly about it.

Since my sisters and I hadn't had anyone caring for us since our mother's death when we were thirteen, I really didn't mind. "We'll drink it. Thank you, Hans."

He nodded, shooing us out. "Come back soon, though! For a proper meal!"

I smiled as I climbed the stairs. Hans really could cook. It was a little weird that he allowed rodents on the counter, but I figured Boris was pretty clean and he always seemed to stay on that one section. I wasn't terribly picky, anyway.

We ate our sandwiches as we crossed the entry hall in silence. I polished mine off as we stepped out into the courtyard. The sun was nearing the horizon, sending a beautiful pink glow over the castle grounds and the mountains beyond.

"So, isn't Pompeii full of tourists?" I asked.

"Part of it is." Lachlan handed me a juice box. He looked at it curiously, as if he only drank whiskey and black coffee, then shrugged and shoved the straw into the little box. "But there's another part—the supernatural district. It's hidden from human eyes, but we'll find our answers there."

Excellent. We could usually count on the good stuff being in supernatural districts. "Do you have a transportation charm?"

He dug into his pocket. "Two left."

I waited as he chucked it at the ground. A cloud of sparkly dust poofed up, and I stepped inside. The ether sucked me in, dragging me across space and spitting me out in Italy. It wasn't much warmer here, though it was darker and the sun now dipped behind the horizon.

It was quiet, and I spun to take in the fields around me. A tall mountain pierced the sky in the distance, looming and dark. Vesuvius.

I shivered, remembering the images of the bodies encased in ash. Vesuvius was a real jerk of a mountain.

Lachlan appeared next to me.

"Where are we?" I asked. I saw no buildings or cars or people. Just a large ruined archway about fifty yards away. It looked ancient.

"We're at the far edge of Pompeii, the part that is hidden."

"Even from supernaturals?"

"Partially. Come on." He set off across the field, walking toward the arch. "This part of Italy is densely populated. To hide the supernatural district of Pompeii, they put a shield over most of it. But we can enter it through here." He pointed up to the huge marble arch that marked the entrance to Pompeii.

I stopped with him and looked up. Two figures appeared at the top of the arch, their short skirts fluttering in the wind. Their helmets concealed their features, and the spears at their sides were as tall as they were.

Roman warriors.

Instant dislike streaked through me, strong and fierce. I shuddered.

What the heck was that about?

It was like one of these guys had kicked a puppy or something, but I'd never met them.

"Who goes there?" they demanded.

I wanted to shout that it was none of their damned business, but it was just my weird emotions talking. Why the heck did I feel like this?

"Belatucadros and his woman," Lachlan shouted back.

I glared up at him. I didn't like the lie—Belatucadros was the Celtic god of war and Bree's boyfriend—and I didn't like being called *his woman*.

He shot me a look that very clearly said *shut up*.

I harrumphed. The guards murmured something, then the heavy iron gates creaked opened. Two more figures stood within, both wearing the same armor as the guards on the top of the arch. Their eyes were cold behind their iron masks, and they raked their gazes over me and Lachlan.

His magic flared, strong and fierce. He might not have been able to use it, but apparently he could still show off his signature like a freaking peacock trying to charm a lady.

One of the guards choked a bit and stumbled back. The other stiffened his spine, but even he looked affected.

"It's him," the stiff guard said.

"Agreed," the other said.

They both stepped back, letting us pass. We walked through the gate, and I stared forward, not daring to look at the guards.

The city that we stepped into was straight out of the past. The stone streets gleamed in the light of the rising moon, and the buildings were all ancient. A forum stretched out in front of us, the open space full of grand buildings fronted with columns. There had to be more than a hundred white columns framing the large rectangular space, and on the far end was an imposing building that looked like the rule of law was determined there.

There were some people in the forum, as well as ghosts who glowed with a gray light.

As soon as we were far enough away from the guards, I hissed, "Why?"

"They wouldn't deny a god entrance."

"I'm friends with Cade, you know," I said.

"Is that what he goes by?"

"Yes. Why him?"

"He's one of the few earth-walking gods. And my magic is strong enough that it can pass for a god's." He grinned like a shark. "So I borrowed his name."

"But what if we cause problems and they track it to him?"

"You think he can't handle it?"

I thought about Bree's boyfriend and the sheer amount of badassery that he possessed. "Fine. He can handle it. Still, I don't like it."

He grinned. "All right. I'll try not to do it again."

"Try?"

He raised a brow. "Try *hard*?"

"Ugh."

We'd passed through the open forum and entered a wide street, so I stopped to look around. Buildings lined either side of the street, which was indented into the ground with raised sidewalks on either side. Water trickled sluggishly down the street, which I supposed was the ancient Roman version of city waste water disposal.

The buildings were one and two stories tall, their bottom halves painted red. I squinted at one. Did the paint mark the old part of the wall, while the paler part above it was the modern addition? Maybe so. There weren't as many windows as in a modern building, but there were inset balconies on many of the second levels.

"Was this place reconstructed?" I asked. "Or did the volcanic eruption not bury it?" The only reason Pompeii was so well preserved was because up to twenty feet of ash and pyroclastic debris had buried it in 79 A.D.

"It was hit by the destruction," Lachlan said. "But it was reconstructed slowly over time. Some of the people who were killed here stayed on as ghosts. Others went on to their afterlives. And other people moved in."

We passed a cell phone shop, and I did a double take. "Didn't expect to see that here."

"The past and the present collide in this part of Pompeii." A man on a Segway scooter zipped by, and a uniformed Roman officer chased after him, shouting. "Though they don't always get along."

I lowered my voice. "Where will we start our search? This place is huge."

"Too huge to work blindly. We'll go to my friend Fabio. He knows the ins and outs of Pompeii."

"You have a lot of friends that know things," I said.

"It's the best way to do business. You can sell more spells that way and avoid selling to those who are unscrupulous."

"So, you don't sell to certain people?"

He shrugged. "Not to warlords, criminals, or suspicious government officials."

"And that's all you do? Make spells and sell them?"

"Occasionally people hire me for dangerous jobs, like this one. Except I'm the one doing the hiring now." He rubbed his chin. "It's quite a switch."

"So, you're like a mercenary?"

"Exactly. Except that I only kill demons. And my price is so high that I don't get offered much work."

"Then lower your price."

"I don't need the work."

Ah, right. Must be nice.

I followed him down several crowded streets, passing more ancient and modern amenities. The place was packed with people—only the forum had been fairly empty, and probably because it was evening. Government was shut down for the day, and so was the market.

We passed by a restaurant with an open front. A woman wearing something similar to a toga was dishing out food from massive terra-cotta pots set into the counter. It smelled savory and delicious, but entirely unfamiliar.

"In the old days, most homes here didn't have kitchens," Lachlan said. "People would eat at taverns like that."

"I think I prefer my place." But I did like the feeling of stepping back into the past—as long as I ignored the cell phone stores.

"We're here." Lachlan turned left, into a large courtyard. Fancy ornamental trees surrounded a fountain, and golden lights lit our path to the front door.

It swung open as we neared, and a short woman grinned at us. Her dark hair was a wild halo around her head. "Lachlan! It has been too long."

"Lilia, how are you?"

"Better now that you are here." She grinned cheekily. "Fabio will be delighted to see you."

I followed Lachlan into another courtyard, but this one had no grass. It seemed like it was the middle of the house, open to the air through a square hole in the ceiling. Beneath the hole, in the middle of the area, was a shallow pool. It was surrounded on all sides by tile floor, with rooms encircling the whole thing.

It pinged a memory of the books I'd read about Pompeii. The size of this place and the layout... It was the home of a rich dude from ancient times. I wondered if they had a homeowner's association here or someone who drove around on a golf cart trying to enforce nitpicky rules about plant placement.

The idea made me giggle, but I swallowed it as soon as a man walked through one of the doors at the back of the courtyard.

His whole aura *screamed* danger. He was the same size as Lachlan, and both looked like they played some kind of professional sport for a living. But his eyes were as cold as a frost giant's butt, and the aura of power that surrounded him competed with Lachlan's. It wasn't quite as strong, but it was enough to make my fingers itch to draw a weapon from the ether.

This guy is on our side.

He strode up to Lachlan, his arms outspread to hug him. Then punched him in the face.

Or tried to.

Lachlan dodged, avoiding the fist by inches.

My heart leapt into my throat.

Lachlan and the man laughed, great booming noises.

Lilia looked at me. "They're idiots."

Lachlan threw a punch this time. The man darted his head away, but Lachlan's knuckles brushed his cheek. The blow left no mark—the man had been fast enough to avoid a real hit—but Lachlan grinned widely. "I win this round."

"Why the hell do you do that?" Annoyance streaked through me. With my job, I pretty much ate violence for breakfast. And I didn't mind it so much. But amongst friends?

I wasn't a fan.

"We met while fighting in the Coliseum," Lachlan said. "It became habit."

"Wait—what? How the heck did you fight there?"

"Saturday night fight rings," the man said. "It's how I made the money to start my business here, and Lachlan did the same. To start his spell peddling business."

"Valuable spells." Lachlan grinned and rubbed his jaw. "I found I got tired of taking a hit to the face that often."

I eyed Fabio. He looked like he spent a lot of time in walk-in freezers, playing Rocky. So yeah, I wouldn't want to spend my Saturdays going one-to-one with him either.

But I was learning a lot about Lachlan. The guy had a varied past, one that dealt primarily in power and violence. Not too far off from my life, but I wasn't sure that was a good thing.

"I'm Fabio." The man held out his hand to shake. His long golden hair glinted in the light, and his grin was charming.

I still didn't really like him—not after the punching—but he wasn't so bad.

I gripped his hand firmly, sizing him up. "I'm Ana Blackwood."

"Of the New York Blackwoods?"

"Of the none-of-your-business Blackwoods." I grinned at him. I had no idea who the New York Blackwoods were. I remembered only my mother, and she'd been gone nearly ten years.

He nodded, clearly getting the picture. "Come. We'll sit, and you can tell me why you're here." He grinned at Lachlan. "And what you need."

"I come to visit for other reasons than just needing something," Lachlan said.

"You don't."

"True."

"It's fine. Ours is not a past to be celebrated." There was something dark in his voice, and the reality of earning your money in gladiator battles hit me.

It had to have been horrible.

I looked at Lachlan with new respect.

This guy was determined, if he'd put up with that crap.

Lilia accompanied us into a room at the back of the house. A large, low table sat in the middle, surrounded by backless couches. They looked more like beds than anything else.

"I see you're still living as the Romans did," Lachlan said.

Fabio flopped onto one of the couches and stretched out. "It's not a bad way to live."

Servants filtered in, laying out platters of food and pitchers of drinks.

"I never understood lying down to eat." Lachlan sat, and I joined him.

No way I was lying down around some guy I didn't know who also happened to scream violence with every move. I needed to be able to jump up and fight if necessary.

"Why are you here, Lachlan?"

I nibbled on some grapes as he explained what we were looking for. I briefly fantasized about dangling the cluster over my head like one of the old cartoons of ancient Rome but nixed it.

When Lachlan finished his description, Fabio nodded. "I think I know where you can go for information. The baths."

I sputtered. "The baths?"

"It's the most popular meeting place in town. Massive, busy, and there are certain sections where the criminal underworld go to do their business. It's been that way for thousands of years, and we Romans like our traditions."

I remembered reading about the baths. They were essentially massive swimming pool complexes where everyone wandered around naked. It was divided by sex, with special rooms for cold baths, tepid baths, and hot baths. It'd be a real blast to the past, but it still wasn't my idea of a good time.

"So it's like a bar, but everyone is naked."

"Indeed."

Now, recon for this job was going to involve stripping down and having a communal bath?

Fabulous.

"Is there any chance that the baths are on Abbondanza Street?"

"They are. How did you know?"

"A hunch."

"Do you have any idea when our target might be at the baths?" Lachlan asked.

"My spies report that they tend to do their business in the evening, after they've completed whatever criminal activity was on the docket for the day."

"So we should go now," I said.

Fabio nodded. "It would be best. I can have a servant direct you there. Once you arrive, tell them that you are my guest. That should gain you access to all areas, even the more elite ones. I can't say where your target will be."

"They have an identifying mark," Lachlan said.

"And since they're naked, we should be able to see it." At least stripping down would have a greater purpose.

10

Since we were going to be spying at the baths, we needed listening devices. I called Jude on my comms charm and explained what the situation was. Within thirty minutes, Hedy arrived, using a transportation stone and apparently charming her way through the gate.

She arrived at Fabio's house dressed in one of her usual long, flowing silver dresses and met us in the room with all the low couches.

She took in the scene, her eyes wide. "This place is amazing. Like I've stepped back in time."

"Isn't it?" I said. I really liked being in a place where the past had come back to life.

"I'm definitely coming back for vacation." Her gaze turned serious. "But I hear you have a lead?"

"We do."

"Good. I've brought two hearing charms." She held out her hand, and two earrings sat there. A glittering gold one and a shiny one that looked like titanium or something. "Hopefully they'll pass as jewelry."

I glanced at Lachlan. He really didn't look like the jewelry type, but he didn't hesitate to clip the charm onto his ear. "Thank you, Hedy."

"Absolutely. Best of luck."

I took the golden charm and clipped it on, saying goodbye to the witch. Then I turned to Lachlan. "Ready?"

He nodded.

Our guide, Kyle, was a slender man in his late twenties. He didn't speak much as he led us through the bustling streets of Pompeii, but I was so busy looking around that I didn't mind the silence.

We passed by numerous bakeries, each of which had its own collection of large hourglass-shaped millstones. They were cranking away even at this hour, grinding the flour for the bread that would bake early in the morning.

On the less savory side of things, there were a lot of people loitering outside the bars, drinking and smoking and having a good time. I was on the receiving end of more leers than normal, which meant that my stink eye got a good workout.

"Busy place at night," Lachlan murmured.

"Seriously. All the life takes place out in the streets."

"Or in the baths."

"So we'll split up? You check out the dude's side; I'll check out the gal's side. And we can meet back at your friend's place once we find something?"

"Good plan."

Our guide stopped in front of an ornately decorated building and swept out his arms. "Here we are."

"Thank you, Kyle," Lachlan said.

We left Kyle and climbed the wide stairs to the entrance. A woman with long black hair and wide dark eyes waited in the entry foyer, which was bigger than my apartment back home.

We stopped in front of her, and Lachlan took over. "We're guests of Fabio Laretti."

She smiled. "Welcome. We're so glad you could come. Would you like the separated baths, or the joined one?"

Separated or joined?

Understanding dawned, and my cheeks heated.

There was a joined one for the people who were modern or brave enough to not mind wandering around naked in mixed company.

I glanced quickly at Lachlan.

I was *so* not ready to see him naked. Not that I wasn't curious —*real* curious—but it would completely fog my mind. I'd be in no state to hunt bad guys.

"We'll start with the separated baths," Lachlan said.

The rest was clear. If we couldn't find our target there, then we'd worry about getting naked together and hunting in the joined section.

I really didn't think I could handle the stress of that. Not gracefully, at least. I would definitely fall flat on my ass while naked. I could already see it.

The woman gave us a few directions—all of which went over my head as I was imagining falling on my ass, naked—then we were off.

Lachlan and I traded one last look, then went through the separate doors that the woman had mentioned. A sign above my doors that was done in a mosaic pattern made of tiny stones read *Apodyterium*.

I had to guess it was the changing room. It turned out that I was right.

And boy, was it *fancy*.

It was laid out roughly like a locker room at a modern gym, but it was built of stone with beautiful frescoes on the walls. Nymphs and animals frolicked all around as women stripped out of their clothes and stacked them in little cubbies. There were people dressed in all manner of clothes, from ancient Roman to modern.

I found a cubby near the entrance to the baths and stripped quickly.

Muffin appeared in front of me, peering around.

This is what humans do for fun?

"I feel you," I muttered. "I'm not so sure myself. But shouldn't you be on the boys' side?"

He gave me a look that said I was an idiot. *I'm a cat.*

"Right, of course." A pile of fluffy towels sat nearby, and I grabbed one and wrapped it quickly around myself. I definitely wasn't used to wandering around naked in front of a whole lot of people. They might not have been looking, but I still liked my security blanket of a towel.

How had the ancient Romans done it?

Then I remembered their public toilets—long benches with holes cut in them. If they could manage that side by side, then they definitely could handle a little public nudity.

As I headed into the first bathing chamber, Muffin trotted alongside me. No one complained, and he was a great body-guard once the claws started flying.

I tried to surreptitiously check out the backs of the other women's necks. Hopefully no one labeled me a creeper, but at least I was keeping my gaze above the shoulders.

A woman walked by us wearing a bikini. Swimsuits were allowed?!

Damn. Would have been nice to know that.

Muffin huffed. *Look at her. She shouldn't be out in a bikini.*

I glanced down at the judgmental little cat. "She looks like an actual supermodel. Her legs went up to her neck, and her boobs totally defied gravity. Like spaceships."

Exactly! Bad for my self-esteem. He wiggled so his little belly jiggled. I laughed, then turned my attention back to the hallway. We were almost to the first room.

I stepped through a doorway into a room that had a huge, round pool. Steps surrounded it on all sides, and women lounged around, talking and resting. A few swam in the middle, but most floated toward the edges, their arms resting on the side of the pool. The ceiling was domed overhead and painted with a beautiful forest scene.

I gripped my towel to my chest and sucked in a deep breath.

Funny how I could fight a dozen demons, but this had me nervous.

Culture was a weird thing, but hard to escape.

Have fun. I'm going to go lick my butt. Muffin trotted off.

I took off the towel and hung it up, then stepped toward the pool.

Hey, this wasn't so bad.

Kinda freeing, actually.

I dipped my toe in and shivered.

The cold bath.

There was no way to avoid it, though. There were so many women in here. Over a hundred, at least. Their voices filtered through the charm at my ear, and I had to focus to separate them out.

Like Fabio had said, most of them were gathered in small groups, talking. I resisted touching the little charm that allowed me to hear them. Hopefully it would pass as an earring and not a listening device.

I submerged fully, then floated around the pool, trying to be sneaky about checking out the backs of other women's necks. With my listening device, I caught snippets of conversation—gossip, lectures, and a few business transactions that sounded like they were worth a lot of money.

They sounded legal, though. Or at least not dangerous. The

selling of massive quantities of a fish sauce called garum and a silver trade. There were a few neck tattoos, but they were the normal sort made of black or colored ink. No silver circles.

Shivering, I climbed out of the cold bath and grabbed my towel, then headed to the next archway. A mosaic sign above read *Tepidarium.*

Muffin trotted over to join me. *I hope this one is warmer.*

"Don't get in," I muttered. I could only imagine the response if the little gremlin jumped into the pool and started swimming around.

I do what I want. And I am a lovely swimmer. He twitched his tail.

This room had a rectangular pool, and most bathers were standing in the middle. On the left side of the room, a band was stationed. It was made up of all women, and they played a variety of instruments, many of which I didn't recognize. The music was unfamiliar, too, but it sounded old. Roman, probably, led by the two ghostly members who had probably played this same music two thousand years ago. The floor was warm underfoot, like they had some kind of heating mechanism down there. I wiggled my toes, starting to enjoy this.

Man, the Romans knew how to party.

It was easier to ditch my towel this time, and the water turned out to be slightly warmer. Tepid.

Unfortunately, my hunt didn't reveal any women with silver circle tattoos who were talking about dangerous business. At one point, I thought I caught sight of a pair of gleaming green eyes in the darkened shadows underneath a marble bench. Muffin was stalking around, hopefully hunting silver circles like I was.

He was helpful, but I prayed Bojangles wasn't here.

I could just imagine him taking a flying leap into the bath.

As I climbed out of the water, I wondered if Lachlan was

having any luck on his side. If our criminals were men, I'd never find them.

Unless they were in the joined section.

I pushed that thought away and picked up my towel. Muffin trotted out to join me. "I can't believe no one minds you being here."

I'm very charming.

I wasn't sure I'd go that far, but I agreed. It wasn't smart to insult a creature who could rub his butt over all of your belongings.

The next room had a round bath. The air and floor were much warmer, and there were nooks cut into the stone walls where one could sit and chat. There were at least one hundred people, and all of the nooks were full.

This looked promising.

I hung up my towel and got in, used to the drill by now. This water was much hotter—like a Jacuzzi. I swam aimlessly, which was kind of weird in the hot water. Almost no one else was swimming, but I had to make the rounds.

As I swam, my hearing charm picked up snippets of conversation, but it was all boring stuff. Love lives, jobs, crappy bosses, a few business transactions.

Then it wasn't so boring at all. I stiffened.

"Where is the drop-off point?" a voice said.

Drop-off point?

Now *that* was interesting.

Slowly, I spun in the water, trying to figure out where the voice was coming from.

In one of the nooks, two women sat. One with dark hair, one with light. Both were leanly muscular, with hard eyes and stern mouths. They looked like they knew how to commit some crimes. One had a bruise all along her jaw, and the other had one on her shoulder.

From fighting?

They were both covered with faded knife scars, many of which looked like my own scars.

Yeah, these ladies knew their way around a demon fight.

Unfortunately, both had long hair that covered the backs of their necks.

But the demons in the Paris sewers had been talking about delivering the spell to a woman.

As subtly as possible, I tried to swim closer. I needed to get a peek at their necks.

"The sorcerer is nearly finished, and *he* wants the spell soon, so I've scheduled the drop," the blonde one said. "It's been hard to evade Lachlan and his goons."

Jackpot!

But goons?

I was no one's goon.

I tried to suppress the scowl and spun in the warm water, trying to act like I was just chilling.

But this water was damned hot. Sweat poured down my temples. I swam toward the side wall of the large pool and climbed up to sit on the submerged bench.

I'd found a lead.

Could I fight them? *Should* I fight them?

No. Though I had weapons in the ether, it'd be better if I didn't alert Lachlan's enemy that we were onto them. They didn't have the spell with them, at least not now, so there was nothing to be gained.

I listened intently.

"My mages are ready to meet at the port tomorrow night," the blonde woman said. "Is your side ready for the drop?"

"They are," the dark-haired one said. "We'll meet at the assigned spot. But he really wants to pick up the spell here?"

"The port is one of the only places where the portal can appear. We have no other choice."

The port.

I stifled a smile. I was onto something here.

Surreptitiously, I peeked at the women, waiting to see if they would say anything else.

The dark-haired woman was staring right at me, eyes curious. When her gaze landed on my ear and narrowed, my heart rate spiked.

Shit.

Time to go.

As casually as I could, I climbed out of the pool, not bothering to go to the official stairs.

"You!" the woman shouted.

"Me?" I tried to look confused. "I sorry—no English."

I prayed she bought my broken accent.

"What the hell is on your ear?"

"I no—" I shook my head, my mind racing.

She climbed out of the water, looking angry as a bull.

"You crazy!" I spun around and walked quickly toward my towel. A shout and a splash sounded, and I glanced behind. The other one had climbed out of the water. A third woman had gotten in their way, it looked like, and they'd shoved her right into the pool.

Holy fates.

I started running. I didn't want to blow my cover and have the drop-off not take place. But how the heck would I do that? Would they even believe that I was just a frightened woman running from them because they were crazy threatening?

How the hell did I preserve the drop-off and not die at the same time?

I sprinted around the pool, naked as a jaybird and way too close to getting hit in the face with my own boobs. I dodged another woman, darting around a group of naked grandmothers, then leapt over a bench.

Muffin was nowhere to be seen.

Could I get them alone and capture them? Force them to do my bidding?

I glanced back. They neared me. There was a green glow around the dark-haired one's hand. *That* looked bad.

It smelled like death, and probably would go a long way toward delivering it.

Ah, shit.

Add *running for my life, naked* to my list of problems. I darted behind a column, panting.

To the left, a blast of green light plowed into the tiled wall. Shards exploded outward. I ducked, covered my face. The tiny ceramic slivers sliced my arms and legs, but I barely felt it. When the worst was over, I peeked. A hole had appeared in the wall, about three feet deep.

Shit.

That woman had some serious magic.

Could my weakened shield stand up to that?

No.

And I definitely couldn't capture them. I was way overpowered.

A shriek rent the air, sounding like the depths of hell had made a baby with a cat.

I peered around the column.

The place had exploded in chaos. All three of the Cats of Catastrophe had arrived. Bojangles was rampaging, his goofy smile wide as he stirred the patrons into a frantic race. Princess Snowflake III had leapt on the dark-haired woman and was going for the throat.

Don't kill her!

I didn't dare scream it—I didn't want them associating me

with these insane beasts, though that may have been a vain hope.

Princess pulled back, her fangs glinting.

It was as if she heard me.

Thank fates.

Muffin hurtled along the ground, then leapt into the air and plowed into the other woman's belly. She crashed backward, arms flailing.

I had an advantage now. Should I try to capture them?

Oh fates, I had no idea.

A dozen burly women rushed into the room, each one wearing a uniform that looked like an ancient Roman version of the police. Their hard eyes swept the room.

My dark-haired nemesis spotted them, her eyes flaring wide. She looked at her friend, who was fighting off Princess Snowflake III, red scratches covering most of her upper body. "Chloe! We have to split!"

They didn't want to get caught by the police.

Which meant I probably didn't want to either.

Chloe threw off Princess Snowflake III and ran for it, darting toward the far exit. The other woman followed.

If I went after them, I'd have to run right by the guards.

Too risky, especially since I didn't know *what* I'd do when I caught them.

So I slipped out the side entrance, my heart pounding. I couldn't go to the dressing room—that was way too far away, and the guards stood between me and it. Magic sparked around them—no way I could get past all twelve.

Cover me! I asked the cats, hoping they could somehow read my mind. Or read the situation, at least.

Bojangles was still going wild, tearing down every towel and knocking every bottle of lotion off the shelves. Normal cat stuff, basically. It was highly effective.

I found a spare towel and wrapped it around myself, then tried to find my way out.

The baths were a maze, and I slipped through a garden and past a public restroom. It was in the ancient Roman style—just one long bench with multiple holes. There were a couple ghosts inside, each sitting on their throne, but no living humans. A ghostly quartet was in the middle of the bathroom, playing a cacophonous melody.

So weird.

"You! Stop!" The voice sounded from behind me.

I glanced back. Guard.

I picked up the pace, racing through the rest of the baths, darting into the men's by accident, then veering out just as quickly. By the time I lost the guards and found a side exit, I was sweating and panting.

So much for getting clean at the baths.

The alley was dark and quiet, and I leaned against the wall, desperately trying to catch my breath.

Holy fates, that had been wild.

A demanding meow sounded at my feet. I looked down.

Muffin stood there, glaring. He had one of my boots gripped in his jaws. At his side, Bojangles held another boot. Princess Snowflake III had brought my T-shirt.

Just my T-Shirt.

Was that intentional?

Whatever. "Thanks, guys."

Fortunately, I'd shoved my socks into my boots, so my feet were comfortable once I'd pulled those on. Then I tugged on my T-shirt and wrapped the towel around my waist.

"How do I look?" I asked the cats.

They looked at me dubiously.

"Lovely," Lachlan said.

I turned to face the exit. Lachlan stood there, perfectly dressed and looking too damned good.

"I take it you had some luck?" he said. "I saw you dart into the men's *caldarium*."

"I had some luck. You?"

"Just seeing you in your towel. Which I count as fairly lucky." His cold eyes weren't so cold anymore. In fact, heat burned in their depths. The grin that softened his lips made me want to lean up and press my lips to his.

Bree was *so* wrong about him being cold. "Let's go before we get caught. I can tell you what I found when we get back."

He nodded, and we hurried through the darkened streets of Pompeii. Fortunately, we met no trouble as we made our way back.

Fabio hadn't waited up for us, but the servant who opened the door got me some fresh clothes. At least I made a habit of not carrying identification with me, so there was nothing of value left in my jeans and leather jacket back at the baths.

Quickly, I changed into the new jeans—which fit amazingly well, surprisingly—then I joined Lachlan out in the sitting room where the servant had brought food and wine.

Exhausted, I flopped down and picked up a glass. I sipped, then scowled.

"It's the old style," Lachlan said. "Not to my taste, either."

"This is what they drank in ancient times?"

"Yes. Fabio is a purist. Now tell me, what did you find? Because there was nothing in the men's baths."

Nothing but a whole lot of naked Lachlan.

Which was really not where my mind should be going.

I ate a bite of bread and cheese as I tried to recall exactly what the women had said. "I didn't see their silver circle tattoos, but they mentioned you by name. And said it was hard to outsmart you and your goons." My brows dropped. "Presumably I'm one of your goons."

"You make an excellent goon."

I wanted to chuck my piece of bread at him, but my tiny well of manners stopped me. This place was way too nice for me to be throwing food. "Anyway, there's going to be a drop-off at a port tomorrow night. They're making a portal, and I think the boss is coming to pick up the spell. A sorcerer had it, but now it's going to its final destination."

"Which port?"

"The one at Pompeii?"

"Pompeii used to have a port, but no longer. The sea line has changed. Now it's just grass near some tourist shops."

"Hmmm. Crap. Not Pompeii's port, then." Disappointment filled me.

"At least they're unlikely to move the location of the drop. If they never said which port, they'll probably doubt you can find it."

"If they thought I was looking. They were just suspicious. They didn't have any confirmation of who I am or what I'm after."

"So we should try to find out which port and ambush their drop-off. It may be canceled, but probably not."

"I bet it'll have extra security, though."

"Which means we should probably have some backup."

"We can ask my sisters. And Caro, Ali, and Haris." I frowned. "But first, we should find out *which* port. I'll call them. Maybe someone else found a clue."

He nodded. "Good."

I touched my fingertip to the comms charm. "Bree? Rowan? Any luck?"

"What's up?" Bree sounded like she'd just finished running a marathon.

"You okay?"

"Just polished off some demons. Getting my exercise in."

"You and Rowan safe?"

"Better than safe. We might have a clue."

"Had to kill some demons to get it, though," Rowan said.

"Ain't easy without magic," Bree added.

"What's your clue?" I asked.

"Found a mage with a silver circle on the back of his neck. He had a plane ticket to Rome, scheduled to leave tomorrow morning."

"Oh, interesting." My mind raced. Rome had to have a big port, right? "That helps."

I told her everything we'd found.

"Excellent," she said. "We're headed back to the Protectorate now. I'll ask Jude if any other teams have found something."

"You read my mind. Thanks, guys."

"Always," Rowan said. "We'll call by tomorrow morning, all right? Hopefully we'll know which port by then."

"Perfect." I hung up and looked at Lachlan.

"That's some good family you have there."

"I'm lucky." I ate a grape and watched him, realizing that I knew so little. "What about you? Family? Friends? Anyone you want to call in to help us tomorrow night?"

He shook his head. "I work alone. Besides Decker, who helps me occasionally. But as you know, he's not available."

"Trying to survive an abduction. Right. Of course." I wanted to ask about family again, but he'd avoided the question. Mildred the ghost had said he had none, so the question was probably better saved for another time. "We'll be fine with this team. And with any luck, we'll catch them in the act. Get the spell, save your friend, and retrieve our magic."

"You don't seem to be too uncomfortable without your magic," he said. "It's not all gone, is it?"

I shrugged. "Maybe the curse missed me."

His brows lowered. "What *are* you?"

"I've told you that plenty of times."

"A garden variety shield mage?" He shook his head. "You're not. Even if you had no other magic, you'd be special."

"Yeah?" I had to admit that I didn't hate hearing it.

He moved closer. "Aye."

I drew in an unsteady breath. Was he flirting with me? Or trying to get info? Either way, I kind of liked it.

But he was dangerous.

The thing was, I didn't really care right now. In fact, I liked it.

I leaned toward him, drawn by the softness of his lips. His cheekbones were sharp as glass, and his eyes hot as molten metal. The scent of him wrapped around me, capturing me in a haze of desire.

Lachlan leaned toward me, seeming pulled by a force that he couldn't fight. His gaze dropped to my lips.

I didn't know who moved first, but in half a second, we were pressed together, his mouth hot against mine. His strong hand cupped the back of my head, and I pressed myself against him, lining my curves up with his harder angles.

His lips were hot and fierce on mine. He kissed as if he were starving, as if he hadn't felt the touch of another in years. He devoured me, making my mind spin and my skin heat.

I moaned against his lips, and he murmured my name.

There was so much desperate want in the single word that I knew it would be imprinted on my mind forever.

No one had ever wanted me this much.

I sank my hands into his hair and licked his lips, trying to get as much of him as possible. He groaned, a raw sound that ripped through me. I was about to push him down on the seat when he pulled back, his gaze torn.

"What's wrong?" I panted, trying to catch my breath.

He looked like he was in agony. "We have to stop. We work together."

What?

Oh crap.

He was right.

My cheeks burned, even as everything in my body screamed at me to kiss him again.

"We can't do this." Gently, he let go of me and stood. His hands fisted at his sides, as if he ached to touch me again, but couldn't.

He was right. Wasn't he?

Either way, this was clearly over for him.

I stood abruptly and nearly tripped over the seat. My face flamed. "Of course. Right. Bedtime for me. See you in the morning."

I fled the room, but my narrow escape felt more like a defeat than a victory. What had just happened?

11

My comms charm blared to life the next morning, Bree's voice interrupting a wildly inappropriate dream about Lachlan.

"Ana? You there?"

"Yeah." I wiped drool off my face and rolled over, falling out of the unfamiliar bed and landing splat on the rug. "Ow."

"Are you okay?" Worry sounded in Bree's voice.

"Fabulous. Just grace incarnate, as usual."

"You fell out of bed?"

Aching, I climbed to my feet. "Nailed it in one. But enough about my glory. Did you find any more clues?"

"Caro did. She was tracking a group of transport mages who said the word Civitavechia."

"What's that?"

"Google says it's the biggest port near Rome."

"Bingo." Between my clue about a meeting at a port, my sister's clue about Rome, and Caro's clue about Civitavechia, we'd figured this out. "Teamwork for the win."

"My kind of victory. Will you head back here first?"

"I don't think we can waste the transport charms. If you'll bring me a change of clothes, we can meet at Civitavechia. But we'll need a team."

"Definitely. I'll talk to Jude."

"It's got to be a huge port, right? If it serves all of Rome."

"Yeah. What are you thinking?"

"I think you should bring the buggy. We'll need it to cover ground fast. Rowan should be done with the engine by now, and I just repaired the stealth feature last week." We'd need to be able to move silently if we wanted to succeed. And if I were being honest with myself, I wanted to get back on the buggy. I missed it.

"Without our magic, we're going to need every advantage we can get," Bree said.

"Seriously." And if we didn't find the answer about the curse when we found the missing spell, we'd be well up a creek.

Later that afternoon, Lachlan and I arrived at Civitavechia. We hadn't spoken about the kiss. It was as if it had never happened. Except for the fact that I replayed it in my mind, over and over. But if he was going to pretend it hadn't happened, so was I.

Easier said than done, however.

Civitavechia was about three hours away by car, so we'd managed to save his last transport stone by borrowing a vehicle from Fabio. It was no buggy, but it wasn't bad. I wasn't the type to complain about a Lamborghini, after all.

Fortunately for me—and unfortunately for Lachlan—I had driven.

He climbed out, slightly shaky and pale, and met my gaze. "I've fought a dozen demons at a time and scaled El Capitan without ropes, but that was something else entirely."

"Aw, don't say my driving scared you."

"Your driving would scare Hercules himself."

I laughed. "I like to go fast. You weren't in any danger."

He grinned, and I kind of wanted to jump on him. "Aye, you're a good driver. But you don't like to go *fast*. You like to go *insanely* fast."

He wasn't wrong.

I inspected the parking lot that I'd chosen—an old employee lot that seemed to be infrequently used—then locked the car and hid the keys under the front wheel so that Fabio could retrieve it.

We hurried toward the meeting point in the southwest corner near one of the large docks. Bree had used a map on the internet to choose the location, and as expected, she waited there with Rowan and her boyfriend Cade. The buggy sat next to them, beautiful in all its intimidating glory.

Their eyes brightened when they saw me. I grinned.

Cade, who was about the size of Lachlan, towered over Bree. His magic smelled like a storm at sea and sounded like clashing swords—appropriate for a Celtic god of war. He was one of the few earth-walking gods, and he wore his power comfortably.

My gaze darted between him and Lachlan. Did Cade realize that Lachlan had been impersonating him?

He didn't seem to, and Lachlan didn't seem bothered. *I'd* be nervous. But not Lachlan. He just stuck out his hand and introduced himself, comfortable as could be.

"Was it hard to get the buggy here?" I asked.

"We had to hire a transport mage since all of ours are affected by the curse," Bree said. "But it worked."

"Thank fates." I petted the front bumper, admiring the repairs I'd made recently.

"I'd think you were happier to see the buggy than us." Bree grinned.

"Never!" I threw my arms around her neck and smacked a kiss on her cheek. Then I pulled Rowan in.

"Enough, enough!" Rowan pulled away.

Shoot. I'd forgotten how easily startled she could be after her time in captivity.

"Sorry," I said.

"Don't worry about it." Rowan turned in a circle to inspect the port, shrugging it off. "This place is massive! It's like a city in itself."

She was right. There were dozens of massive docks, thousands of shipping containers piled up like towers, and cranes everywhere. It was a nautical industrial mishmash. The place was closing down for the night, but during the day, I had a feeling the sound of new construction was cacophonous.

Bree held out a plastic bag. "A change of clothes."

"Thank you." I took it gratefully, then found a quiet corner between some shipping containers. It smelled a bit weird, but it did the job.

Once I was changed, I returned to my sisters. They were interrogating Lachlan, while Cade watched with a grin on his face. He'd once been interrogated and passed. Is that what Rowan and Bree were thinking? That Lachlan would become my Cade?

I had no idea what to make of that, so I shoved the thought away. I caught snippets of the conversations, latching on to words like *for a living, your family,* and *intentions.*

Intentions?

Towards me?

I ambled up, glaring at Bree and Rowan. They shrugged.

To Bree's left, the air began to shimmer. I pointed to it. "Incoming."

Bree moved right, and a second later, Caro appeared out of

thin air, her bright platinum hair gleaming in the light of the setting sun. She darted out of the way of the portal, and Ali stumbled through next, followed by Haris. Each wore a heavy bag slung over his back, no doubt full of potion bombs since they couldn't use their magic. The djinns would normally possess someone, while Caro would fight with high-powered water jets, but they were as powerless as the rest of us now.

"Hey!" Caro said. "Perfect timing."

"I just hope we're in the right place," I said.

A few more people arrived through the portal, Jude and Hedy among them.

Jude's gaze met mine. "What's your plan?"

The slightest bit of apprehension shivered over my shoulders, but excitement followed. This was a chance to prove myself. If she didn't like my plan, she'd no doubt veto it. But giving me a chance to run this operation was a huge step.

I took a deep breath and laid out my idea.

As soon as it was full dark, we put my plan in motion. Jude had liked it—jackpot!—and now all we had to do was make sure it ran flawlessly.

No problem.

Ha. As if.

But I had my sisters and friends at my back, along with Lachlan. I wasn't sure if he could be called a friend, but in a fight, I was glad to have him at my side.

"Ready?" Rowan asked.

"Yep." I climbed up onto the buggy, then jumped into the driver's seat.

Our plan was to use the buggy to search the massive port for our targets. We had a dozen Protectorate members taking their positions around the port. They were perched on top of cranes and towers of shipping containers, getting as high as possible to get a good view of any activity. Using comms charms, they'd direct us where to go.

Bree and Rowan climbed onto the front fighting platform. It covered the hood of the car and was surrounded by a single railing to keep them from flying out when I made crazy turns.

Cade and Lachlan took the back platform, while Caro jumped onto the bench seat next to me. She could stand and fight from there—every spot on the buggy was a fighting spot. Ali and Haris took the back seat, crowded in with a pile of shields that we'd probably end up needing in a fight.

Jude stood on the ground, catching my eye. "Good luck, Ana."

"Thanks." I sucked in a steady breath.

Please let me be right about this.

Sure, I wanted to ace the Academy. Though *ace* was a bit generous. I'd settle for passing.

But there was way more at stake here. This would be our last chance to retrieve the spell—I could feel it. We'd had two near misses now, and they were about to hand the magic off to the person who had bought it.

We couldn't fail.

"Harnesses!" I said. "Safety first!"

Bree grinned at me, then snapped the climbing harness around her waist. It was attached to the railing surrounding the platform and was our version of a seat belt.

As soon as everyone was buckled in, I hit the stealth button. Then I cranked the key in the ignition. It was as silent as an electric car, but I could feel it rumble under me.

I pressed on the gas and took off, trying to recall my memory of the map of the port. Caro had a cell phone just in case we needed to use GPS.

"Testing, testing." I touched the comms charm at my neck.

"Katie here."

"Jude here."

"Hedy here."

All of the team members who were perched around the port reported in. Most had binoculars, though a lucky few were wearing Hedy's eyesight enhancement charms.

I drove relatively slowly through the darkened port. It was a maze of tiny roads through the piles of shipping containers. I kept my senses alert, feeling for any signs of dark magic.

"There are so many hiding places," Caro muttered.

"I know. It's crazy." Every nook and cranny could contain a guard or a demon. The hair on my arms stood up. How many would they bring for this operation?

"Ana?" Hedy's voice echoed out of the comms charm. "I see some activity in the northwest corner. Can't say for certain what it is."

"Thanks, Hedy." I turned left, having a vague instinct where the northwest corner was located. "Caro?"

"On it." She pulled out her phone and began to give directions.

The atmosphere in the buggy was tense as we prowled through the alleys created by the shipping containers. They loomed tall overhead, blocking out what little light there was.

"On your tail!" a voice sounded from my comms charm. "Coming up strong. Look out!"

It was Jude. She must be above us, sitting on one of the cranes. I didn't dare look back. "Hear that, guys?"

"Aye," Lachlan said.

The sound of a low growl sounded, making my skin go cold.

On the front platform, Bree turned around. All the blood rushed from her face.

Ah, hell.

I caved, glancing in the rearview mirror.

I nearly screamed.

12

A massive monster ran behind us, gaining speed as it approached. Fangs the size of steak knives filled the beast's mouth. It was shaped roughly like a mutant dog, but the similarities ended there. Scales covered the creature's body, and its eyes burned like hellfire.

"What is it?" Fear shivered in Caro's voice.

"No idea." My heart thundered as the footsteps pounded behind us. "But we're definitely in the right place, because he's a guard dog if I ever saw one."

"Potion time," Ali said.

I divided my attention between the road ahead and the rearview mirror.

Ali and Haris climbed onto the back platform, handing out potion bombs to Lachlan and Cade, who had sheathed their swords. The beast was only twenty feet off now. They hurled their bombs. The colorful glass spheres flew through the air and exploded against the beast's hide.

It stumbled, then righted itself, plowing after us. Its footfalls shook the ground. I could feel it, even through the buggy.

"I knew I should have put spikes on the back of the buggy," I muttered. Coated with ravener poison, they'd have paralyzed the beast.

"Next time," Bree said as she climbed onto my seat, then scrambled into the back. Rowan followed, her face pale but determined.

My gaze darted between the road and the fight. The guys were hurling bombs, but the monster kept coming!

Crap.

I pressed on the gas, driving as fast as I dared through the narrow passages.

"Turn left!" Caro said.

"Hang on, guys!" I veered left, driving along the massive dock. A huge tanker was tied up next to us, looming ten stories overhead. The scent of dark magic rolled over me.

We were on the right track.

I swerved around a massive pile of ropes, sparing a second to glance back at my friends.

The monster was so close that its face filled my rearview mirror. My friends were hurling potion bombs as fast as they could, but they clearly weren't penetrating the hide of the massive beast.

Then it happened, so quickly that I almost didn't realize what was going on. Lachlan unsnapped his harness, then leapt off the back of the truck, right onto the monster's head. He barely avoided its jaws, grabbing onto the horns and pulling himself onto the top of the creature's skull.

He wrapped his strong legs around its neck, then called his sword from the ether and plunged his blade into the back of the creature.

Holy fates!

I glanced forward just in time to see another huge pile of rope. I swerved, barely avoiding it, my heart thundering in my ears.

"A little warning!" Bree cried.

I looked back in the mirror in time to see the monster stumble and fall, the scent of dark magic exploding out from it. The reek of garbage made my eyes water.

Lachlan jumped off the creature just as it exploded in a poof of black dust.

I slowed the buggy briefly, giving him enough time to race back to it and jump on.

My mind spun as my friends congratulated him.

Lachlan had had no magic and no backup, and *still* he'd jumped right at the jaws of that great monster. If the beast had had quicker reflexes, it could have jumped up and bit him straight through the middle.

"That's one crazy guy." Jude's voice echoed through my comms charm.

"No kidding. Any more of those beasts coming up?"

"No, that's the only one I saw. But you're getting pretty close. I imagine they'll have set up guards around the periphery, just in case—"

A flash of movement flying through the air ahead made me lose track of Jude's words. A figure leapt from the top of the barge and landed in front of the buggy with a thud.

A demon, at least ten feet tall and built like a Mack Truck stood in front of us.

"Crap!" Caro said. "I don't have my magic, and I can't throw to save my life."

And everyone else was in the back. "Grab the wheel!"

She took it, and I scrambled onto the front platform and drew my blades from the ether. I hurled the first one, nailing the demon in the chest. No blood sprayed, and somehow, he kept standing.

Then he started running, pounding toward me on massive feet. He wore heavy armor that glinted in the light of the moon. My blade stuck out of his chest, but he didn't seem to feel it.

He was twenty yards off and gaining.

I threw another dagger, hitting him just under the throat. He stumbled, then threw out his hand. A blast of flame hurtled toward us.

"Swerve!" I screamed, holding on.

Caro jerked the wheel, and the buggy veered right. But it wasn't far enough. I called upon the dregs of my magic, envisioning a shield. It sputtered to life, deflecting the worst of the flame. Then it died.

But I was ready.

I chucked another blade, hitting him square in the middle of the throat. He was so close to the buggy that the spraying blood hit me in the chest. Caro jerked the wheel again, barely avoiding running him over.

"We have to be close!" Bree said.

"There's activity up ahead!" Jude's voice sounded from my comms charm. "A lot of magic just lit up the night!"

Rowan climbed onto the front platform with me, her dark hair whipping in the wind. I glanced back to see that Bree had taken the wheel, then turned to face whatever was coming.

"Right!" Caro called.

Bree turned, driving away from the dock. We weaved through towers of shipping containers. When demons began to jump off the towers, I knew we were close.

I drew my dagger and threw, aiming for a demon in front of us. It sliced him through the eye, and bile rose in my throat. That was my weak spot. I hated an eye shot.

My friends hurled daggers and potion bombs, taking out the demons who leapt down at us. One landed on the platform between Rowan and me. She was fast, stabbing it through the back, then grabbing it by the collar and heaving it over the side of the platform. The motion was practiced and smooth.

"Holy fates, you're fast!" I said.

She looked at me, eyes bright. "I've been practicing."

I knew she'd been obsessed with weapons training lately—she'd been living without her magic for longer than me—but she was seriously badass.

We took out a dozen more demons, then they stopped entirely. Up ahead, the piles of shipping containers stopped, too. It was like looking down a narrow alley that opened up to a large street. There was a clearing at the end, and it stank of dark magic. I breathed shallowly, nearly vomiting from the stench.

Magic glowed from the clearing. "Jude, I think we've found it."

"I'm sending in backup."

Bree slowed the car to a prowl. I turned around, and Caro handed me one of the shields we'd loaded into the truck. Everyone else grabbed one, and I turned to face forward, bracing myself.

"Backup will be there in two minutes," Jude said. "But you'd better get in there. The magic is growing."

"On it." Bree stepped on the gas.

I braced myself against the stench.

When the buggy rolled out into the clearing, I got my first good look at what we were up against.

Eight mages stood in a circle, each guarded by two or three demons. They were facing the center of the clearing, where the rubble of an ancient site stood derelict. Fallen columns surrounded piles of stone. Magic radiated out from the place, old and powerful. The mages directed their magic at the ruins—trying to create a portal?

I'd put money on it.

This was why they were here. Something about the ruins made it possible to create the portal they needed.

The women that I'd seen in the baths were here as well, guarded by a half dozen demons. One had a satchel over her shoulder. It glowed with power. I glanced back at Lachlan. His gaze was glued to it.

"That's the spell?" I asked.

"Aye."

I turned to face them again. They'd all noticed us but hadn't moved. Sweat rolled down the mages' faces as they fed their magic to the ruins, frantically trying to create the portal. The demons guarding them crouched low, some drawing weapons. The others raised their hands to throw magic at us.

"Evacuate!" I called.

The buggy was too big a target, and we had no super shields. If they hit us with a huge fireball or lightning blast, we'd all be toast, and the mission would fail.

Everyone bailed out of the buggy and rolled away just as a massive fireball plowed toward it. It smashed into the front of the truck, the heat blazing out to the side and singeing my skin. I sprinted away, cursing.

The reinforced bumper and hood kept the buggy from exploding in a fireball, but the front looked seriously damaged.

No time to worry about that.

I scrambled upright and chose my target. Lachlan was already headed toward the two women with the spell. He ran like a man possessed, sure strides carrying him across the clearing. I darted after him, while my friends split up and headed for the mages.

If we could take some of them out, they couldn't make the portal, and the spell could never leave.

Bree and Rowan joined me, their shields raised.

We hadn't even reached the line of demon guards before two

of them hurled fireballs at us. I knelt and raised my metal and rubber shield, huddling behind it and wishing my magic were more reliable.

The fireball smashed into my shield and sent me skidding back in the dirt. I barely stayed upright on my knees, though the rubber-like lining on the inside of the shield protected me from the heated metal.

"Are you all right?" Bree cried.

"Yeah!" As soon as the flame died, I peered around the shield and caught sight of a fire demon. His burnished red skin glowed with an unholy light.

He was powering up his flame, which bought me a second.

I hurled my dagger at him. He glanced up, his eyes widening, and flung out his hand, then jerked it to the side. The blade deflected at the last minute, flying left. It sliced him across the arm, then flew harmlessly away.

"Fire and telekinesis." That was bad news.

Ahead of us, Lachlan slammed his shield against one of the mage's heads. He'd gone the brute-force route and plowed straight through the fireballs, his insane strength keeping him on his feet.

All around us, my friends fought the demons who guarded the mages. Ali and Haris fought in a team, as usual, while Caro was a whirlwind with her sword, platinum hair flying.

Reinforcements arrived, joining them, but the demons were strong.

I drew another dagger from the ether and hurled it at a pale blue demon who was about to throw an icicle toward Lachlan. It pierced the demon in the chest, and he staggered backward.

"Incoming!" Rowan called.

Another fireball flew my way, and I raised my shield again. The force of the blast nearly sent me off my feet. As soon as it dissipated, I got up and charged, drawing my sword from the ether.

I couldn't give him time to recoup his power. As I neared, his skin glowed brighter.

Crap! He was almost powered up.

He raised a hand to hurl a fireball, but I dived low, swiping out with my blade.

I barely reached him, slicing a thin line across his shins. He howled, stumbling, and I jumped to my feet. He swung out with one big fist. I raised my shield, but I was too slow. He nailed me in the arm, and my grip slackened. The shield dropped to my feet.

I ignored the pain as I swung my sword, aiming for his neck.

He dodged, fast for such a big demon.

I followed, stabbing with my blade. The steel sank into his side. He howled and tried to jerk backward, but his leg wounds made him awkward.

I twisted the blade, then kicked him in the stomach, dislodging him from my sword.

Bree and Rowan had each taken out a demon, and Lachlan had taken out two. There were still five more to go, though.

All around, demons had fallen. Even some of my friends. But the mages were still working.

Magic filled the air, dark and powerful. I stole a glance at the portal.

It shimmered with a silver light, then a figure appeared. Panic flared in my chest, making my heart race.

The figure was draped in a heavy, hooded cloak that seemed to absorb all light. Dark magic flowed out from it, sending a streak of cold fear right through my middle.

Oh no.

The demons who protected the two women charged us. Two collided with Bree and Rowan, and three of them leapt on Lachlan. One lunged for me, but I ducked, avoiding his blow.

The two women sprinted by me, headed for the portal. I lunged, trying to grab the glowing satchel, but she was too far away.

They raced toward an escape, taking the spell with them.

Oh, *hell* no.

I sprinted after them.

They were fast, nearly to the portal. The cloaked figure waited for them, his impatience obvious from the way he shifted. I pushed myself, running as fast as I ever had. My lungs burned and my breath heaved.

All around, the battle raged, but our side was losing.

Desperately.

The women leapt into the portal.

Then all three disappeared.

No!

I was only feet away. So close.

The portal still glowed.

I leapt into it.

This was the most dangerous thing I could do. Stupid, really. It was common knowledge that jumping into unknown portals was basically a death sentence.

But we had no way to track the spell from here.

Right before the ether sucked me in, I heard Rowan scream. "Ana! No!"

Then the ether sucked me up and spun me around, carrying me on a wild ride through space. It was worse than normal, way more chaotic, and my stomach heaved.

When it spit me out into a dark forest, my head whirled. I fought the nausea as I frantically scrambled toward a pile of boulders, seeking a hiding space.

They didn't know that I'd followed them.

If they found out, I was dead.

I huddled in a small space between two rocks, holding my breath as I took in my surroundings. Twisted old trees surrounded a ruined Roman temple in front of me. The portal had arrived right in the middle of the fallen column. Maybe they used the magic of the temple to make the mega portal? Probably.

I squeezed my eyes shut and focused on my hearing, but I couldn't hear the three who had gone before me—just the rustle of the leaves and the hooting of an owl. The night was dark, illuminated by just a sliver of the moon that revealed twisted old trees and a few boulders scattered here and there.

The portal glowed with a faint gray light, and I waited.

No one else came through, and it faded.

I swallowed hard.

Holy crap, I was alone.

Adrenaline made my muscles tremble as I rose slowly, peeking over the tops of the boulders to find my targets.

I peered through the woods, finally catching sight of three figures walking toward the moon.

"Ana! Where the hell are you?" Rowan's voice sounded loud and clear.

I slapped a hand over the comms charm and crouched down. "Shhhh!"

"Damn it, Ana! It's too dangerous." Lachlan's voice hissed out of the comms, but it was quiet, at least.

"You can't—" Bree's voice was cut off by a scream, then a curse.

Panic flared inside me—for Bree and myself. I touched the charm, killing the connection briefly. I popped up, peeking over the top of the boulder to see if the three figures had heard me.

They kept walking, farther away. Thank fates.

I ducked back down again and touched the charm. "Bree!

Rowan!" I whispered." Are you okay?"

There was nothing.

They *always* answered. Even if it was just to tell me to buzz off if they were busy.

The fight must still be raging, and we'd been losing when I left.

Fear like I'd never known froze my muscles. *Not my sisters.*

I couldn't lose my sisters.

I sucked in a ragged breath. *Get ahold of yourself.*

As quietly and quickly as I could, I left the shelter of the boulders and followed the three figures. I couldn't lose this spell. *Especially* if the Protectorate lost this battle. Maybe I could even use it to save my sisters, somehow.

I shook the thought away.

They'd be okay. I wouldn't need to save them.

They were great fighters. Lachlan was a great fighter. And so were all my friends at the Protectorate. They would make it out. Then they could come find me. Bree and Rowan had the tracking charms that linked the three of us. We'd had them for years, a safety precaution due to our lifestyle.

I ignored the fact that they didn't always work and set off after my targets.

As I hurried silently through the forest, I tried to take stock of my magic. It was inside me, faint as usual, but I had at least a little bit. I gave my targets a good lead, hanging back far enough that I hoped they couldn't hear me. The trees and boulders provided some cover, but when we reached an open field, I faltered.

Crap.

There was no way to sneak across that.

The three had already started walking through the field, which was a dormant vineyard. In the distance, a large manor house sat on a hill.

They were headed there. Maybe I needed to give them some time to make it all the way across, then I could sneak in?

But what if—

Pain exploded in the back of my skull, and I staggered forward, going to my knees.

"The boss won't be happy about this," a voice grumbled.

Stars floated in front of my eyes, and my head felt like it'd been split in two. Groggy, I rolled over and looked upward. There were four figures surrounding me, all of them demons. They were blurry though.

One poked me with his toe. And by poke, I meant kicked.

I grunted and squeezed my eyes shut. When I finally opened them, the four figures coalesced into two. Okay, so I had double vision.

That wasn't good.

In fact, everything about this scenario wasn't good.

"We'll just have to bring her to him," one of the demons said.

They were both a dark gray color, with large horns and fangs that extended past their chins. Ragged leather vests covered their wide chests, but no weapons hung from them.

Smoke demons, I had to bet.

I tried to scramble to my feet, but one of them kicked me again, right in the stomach.

Pain flared and I curled in on myself. Before I could straighten and try again, one of the demons picked me up and slammed me over his shoulder. Agony flared again, and I nearly puked on him.

I almost wished I had.

They carted me off through the vineyards, running at a slow jog that was misery on my stomach. I tried to take in the details around me, but it was just leafless vines and piles of dirt.

Would my friends be able to track me? Or was I screwed?

13

B y the time we made it to the manor house, I was pretty sure I'd take death over another ten minutes over this demon's shoulder.

Where were the Cats of Catastrophe when I needed them?

From far away, I hadn't seen that the manor house was surrounded by a wall. It was at least twenty feet tall and seven feet thick—more suited to a castle than a winery. The demons carried me through the massive iron gate into a beautiful courtyard. It was all upside down from my perspective, but it was pretty.

Fountains burbled in the moonlight, and a carefully planned garden bloomed with flowers. That had to take some serious magic, since it was the middle of the winter.

For fates' sake, that really wasn't important right now.

I already knew these folks were mega-powerful. But all the blood rushing to my head seemed to make me stupid.

The demons carried me around the back of the manor, which had to contain twenty rooms, at least. Maybe more. I wasn't good at judging size on large houses. We went through a heavy door and down some stairs. I caught sight of some enormous wine barrels, right before they chucked me into a cell and slammed the door.

"I hope we get a reward for her," one of the demons said as he ambled away.

I scrambled up and grabbed the bars of my cell, peering out.

The cellar was dark and silent. Rows of enormous barrels watched me, silent sentries. There were no guards, at least that I could see, but my cell was locked tight.

I tugged on the bars anyway, because hope springs eternal, right?

Of course it didn't work.

I sat back on my butt. "Shit."

There had to be a way out of here. But first, I needed to know how my sisters were doing. I touched my comms charm. "Bree? Rowan?"

Silence.

Shit.

My stomach sank to the bottom of the earth as worry crawled over my skin like a spider. I sucked in a deep breath, trying to keep the tears at bay.

This cell was no problem.

Being captive was no problem.

My sisters not picking up their comms charms—even just to scream at me that they were busy?—*that* was a possible problem.

I sucked in another ragged breath and muttered, "Suck it up, buttercup."

The sound of a fight echoed from somewhere else in the building. Then a muffled scream.

I surged upright, grabbing the bars and trying to get a peek. My heart thundered.

What was going on?

Then the Cats of Catastrophe strolled into view. Princess

Snowflake III had blood streaked from her mouth all the way down her white chest. The diamond nestled in her fur looked more like a ruby.

Whoever had just been screaming had clearly gotten on the wrong side of her.

Bojangles was gallivanting around, while Muffin strode straight to the cell, Snowflake following at his heels. He meowed loudly, and Bojangles's head jerked up. He followed Muffin into my cell, all three cats slipping through the bars.

Quickly, they took up position. Princess Snowflake III stood near the door's lock, then Bojangles jumped on her back. Muffin completed the pyramid by jumping onto Bojangles. He then stuck his skinny, hairless tail into the large keyhole and wiggled it around some.

The lock clicked, and the door swung open.

"Wow. Thanks, guys."

They meowed.

"Is this how you run your jewel heists?"

Princess Snowflake III shot me a look to suggest that those were *much* more sophisticated operations.

Muffin meowed. *This is child's play.*

"Sorry." I held up my hands. "Didn't mean to offend."

I peered out. "You guys have any idea where the spell is? Or another prisoner?"

All three shook their heads.

"Then let's get searching."

I stuck to the shadows in the wine cellar, hiding behind barrels and large, unrecognizable machines. I had to assume they made wine, and that the operation was pretty enormous, given the size of this place. I was about to search a smaller room when my comms charm blared to life.

"Ana?" a voice whispered.

"Bree! Are you okay?"

"Yeah, little beat up. But okay."

"Rowan?"

"Good too. And Lachlan."

How had she known that I was about to ask about him? Sister intuition, no doubt.

"There were no casualties, though there were some mean injuries," she continued. "Ali will be out for a while, but he'll recover. Now where are you?"

"You can't find me using the tracking charms?" It'd helped her rescue me before, when I'd been abducted by a miserable mob boss out to steal my blood for some kind of horrible spell.

"There's a shield where you are. Powerful magic. It's totally blocking the tracking charm."

No surprise. Should have thought of that when I jumped through that portal.

"Damn it, Ana. It was too dangerous!" Rowan's voice piped in.

"I'm fine, guys. They caught me, but I escaped."

"Damn right you did," Bree said. "That's what Blackwoods do."

"And now we're going to rescue you," Rowan said. "Where are you?"

"A massive vineyard with a very big manor house on a hill."

"Tuscany, perhaps," Lachlan said. He must've been speaking very close to the charm around someone's neck.

"I'll find a way to tell you more precisely," I said.

"This is one of those times where it'd be handy if you had a cell phone," Bree said.

"True." We'd never been able to afford the things, and now that we had jobs with real salaries—even trainees at the Academy got a little stipend—I found I didn't want a cell. *Buuuut* it'd be real handy to pop open the GPS on one of those babies right about now. "I'll find one. Then I'll look for Lachlan's friend and the spell."

"Give us your location first." Worry sounded in Lachlan's voice. "You'll never manage alone."

"Burn," I muttered.

"Just be careful," he said.

I still thought I detected a bit of worry, but that wasn't something I should even care about anyway.

"Bye, guys," I said. "I'll get you coordinates soon."

I touched the charm to disengage the magic, then re-scouted my surroundings. Still quiet, thank fates. Bojangles was trying to break into a cask of wine, and it looked like he was about to be successful. As soon as he pulled that massive cork out of the side of the barrel, he'd go flying when the wine shot out.

"Bojangles, quit!"

At that second, he managed to dislodge the cork. As expected, a powerful stream of red wine came gushing out. Still clinging to the giant cork, Bojangles went flying across the room.

Crap!

Princess Snowflake III and Muffin rushed over to the wine and began lapping it up. Muffin looked like a regular at a shady bar, and Princess Snowflake III was a real sight with her blood-stained chest and red-wine-covered face.

"No getting wasted!" I hissed. "We have a job to do."

Princess Snowflake III gave me an annoyed look, but Muffin stopped drinking. On the other side of the room, Bojangles was covered in red wine, but he didn't look like he minded.

"Come on!" I raced away from the scene of destruction, hoping that no one had heard the barrel pop.

About forty feet away, I found another hiding spot behind a giant machine of unexplainable usage. The cats followed me over.

"I need to find a cell phone," I whispered. "You guys are thieves. Can you sniff one out?"

Muffin gave me a disdainful look. *Sniff out a cell phone?*

"Is that not how it works?"

We're not bloodhounds. We're internationally acclaimed jewel thieves.

I frowned. "Fine. Let's go."

I crept between the barrels, searching for a guard or a demon or anyone, really. The wine cellar was an ancient, stone-lined labyrinth, and a few times I found other cells built into nooks and crannies in the wall.

"Multipurpose, huh?" I muttered to the cats as we snuck around a section of smaller barrels. "Make some wine, torture some prisoners!"

A few minutes later, I came to a door. There was a little window set into the wood. I didn't dare stick my head up there, in case someone was looking. My head was way too big.

I looked down at the cats, then grabbed Muffin and picked him up. "You look, okay?"

He flattened his ears down, and I raised him up. He peeked briefly, then squirmed wildly. *Demon!*

Oh crap!

I drew my sword from the ether and yanked the door open. Princess Snowflake III leapt onto the demon's belly, claws outstretched. Surprise flared in his eyes as he raised the blade clutched in his fist.

Fast as I could, I stabbed my sword through his neck, ducking to avoid the blood spray. It splattered on the wall behind me. At this range, I'd have preferred a less messy chest shot, but he couldn't be allowed to scream.

He collapsed, Princess Snowflake III riding him down to the ground like he was a sinking ship. She leapt off at the last moment, clearly not wanting to eat him. Which I was grateful for.

Eat him? Muffin looked at me like I was insane.

Princess Snowflake III ignored me.

There was no one else in the little room, thank fates. Small and stone-lined, it seemed to be some kind of storage space for special bottles.

I dropped to my knees at the demon's side and patted his pockets, praying that he'd been on earth a long time. Long enough to want a cell phone. Not that he could get one through the magical dealers, but the mage who hired him could. They often did, for those demons who worked for them long enough. Comms charms were hard to come by.

When I patted a lump by his hip, I grinned, then stuck my hand into his pocket and yanked out a shiny black cell phone.

"Jackpot!" I whispered.

At my feet, the demon's body began to disappear back to the underworld. With any luck, he'd be gone before anyone realized I'd killed him.

I took my prize back to the shelter of some of the wine barrels and poked at the screen, swiping with my thumb. After a few seconds of fiddling, the thing turned on. It took longer to pull up the maps application since I was so unfamiliar, but eventually I got a latitude and longitude.

"Bree? Rowan? I've got something." I rattled off the coordinates.

"Good. We should be there soon," Rowan said.

"There's a huge wall. Call me when you arrive. I can meet you, and hopefully I'll have found a good way in."

"Will do. Stay safe."

I cut the connection, then powered down the phone and stuck it between two loose stones in the ancient wall. I almost considered taking it, but the demon's master could have tracked it. And I didn't want a dead demon's phone anyway.

"Come on, guys. Let's go find Lachlan's friend Decker and retrieve the spell." I set off, not sure if the cats were following me. They'd show up if I really needed them, I was starting to believe.

I'd covered almost the entire enormous wine cellar when a voice sounded from about twenty feet away, back in the far corner.

"Hey, lady, who are you?"

I squinted into the dim light, catching sight of an arm sticking out of a cell door. I hurried forward, spotting a skinny young man with big dark eyes. A swash of dark hair flopped over his forehead in a trendy style, and his band T-shirt was dirty and ragged. He looked hungry and tired, and bruises speckled his jaw.

His eyes widened when he saw me. "Ana?"

"Connor? What are you doing here?" I hadn't seen him in a month. We didn't know each other well, but we had mutual friends in Cass, Del, and Nix, the FireSouls who'd been too busy to help Lachlan because of an emergency.

Holy crap, *this* had to be the emergency.

"Well, you know. Just being a prisoner. The usual." His English accent was strong despite the fact that he'd lived in Magic's Bend, Oregon for about a decade. "It's not as fun as making lattes and potions, but it'll do."

I looked around for the cats and spotted them nearby, trying to pry a silver medallion off a large wine barrel. "Guys, you gotta get my friend out of here."

The cats ran over and got to work with their unlocking routine, and I looked back at Connor. He worked at Potions & Pastilles in Magic's Bend, the coffee shop he and his sister owned. On the side, he made potions. "You're friends with Lach-lan, right? Abducted while helping him?"

"I am."

"But why did he call you Decker?"

"That's my last name."

"So I didn't know I was looking for you this whole time because of some cool-guy thing, like going by your last name?" I'd thought I was rescuing a stranger, when in reality I was rescuing my *friend*. I'd never known Connor's full name. Apparently, I should have asked.

Now I *really* had to get us out of here alive.

He grinned. "Basically."

"Ugh. Dudes."

Muffin wiggled his tail in the lock, and it popped open. Connor stepped out. "Can you get a message to my sister and the FireSouls? I bet they're worried sick. I don't know why they haven't found me yet."

"This place is blocked with powerful magic. Tracking charms don't work, so I'm sure that the FireSouls' tracking power is blocked too. It took the whole Protectorate to find this place." I touched the comms charm at my neck. "Bree? Can you get a message to the FireSouls that Connor is here with me?"

"Wait, what? Connor?" Shock sounded in her voice.

"Apparently, he's Decker. That's his last name."

"Well, crap. Yeah, I'll tell them. They'll be good fire power."

"Thanks. See you soon. We're off to look for the spell."

Bree and Rowan both spoke at the same time. "Be careful."

I cut the comms charm, and Connor grinned at me. "You've got backup coming?"

"Soon. In the meantime, we need to find the *ancientus* spell that was stolen and also whatever magic is suppressing the power of the Protectorate members who are hunting it."

"I can help you with the second part," he said. "I heard the guards talking about a huge dampening spell that the Creeper is running. It's separate from the *ancientus* spell, but I think we can take it out."

"The Creeper?"

"I don't think that's his real name. But I've heard mention of a lair down by the lake."

"Great, let's go before any guards show up."

We set off through the cellar, looking for the door.

"How'd you end up here if the *ancientus* spell only just arrived?" I asked. "Weren't you captured while transporting it?"

"Yeah. But the spell had to go to a sorcerer to be decrypted."

"Decrypted?"

"Of course. Did you think that Lachlan was sloppy enough to let such a dangerous spell out into the wild?"

"Um, maybe?"

"Well, he's not. He put a powerful encryption on it so that only the intended recipient could use it. There's just a few sorcerers in the world powerful enough to break an encryption like that."

"And I suppose the evil mastermind who built this place knows a guy like that?"

"Or can hire one. I don't know the details—this is really just all assumption and bits and pieces I picked up."

"It makes sense, though." I stopped in front of the door that I was pretty sure was the exit. Everything had looked different when I'd been hanging upside down over the shoulder of a demon. "Do you know where the lake is?"

He shook his head. "I've only heard them talk about it."

"No problem. We'll find it." If we could manage it before my friends arrived, they'd have their magic back in time to help us retrieve the *ancientus* spell.

Slowly, I pushed open the door and peeked outside. The moon hung high overhead, and fortunately it was just a sliver.

There was only one guard patrolling—a demon, from the looks of those horns. He was about fifty yards away, pacing near the great wall that surrounded the manor. Almost out of range.

Almost.

I drew a dagger from the ether and got him in my sight, then threw. The blade flipped end over end, glinting in the pale moonlight, before it sank into his back.

He stumbled forward and fell flat on his face, then lay still.

"Blimey, you're good at that."

"Thanks." I continued to scout the grounds, but no one else came. I didn't see a lake, either.

Hopeful, I tried calling on my magic. It sputtered weakly inside me, still clearly influenced by the spell that was affecting everyone at the Protectorate.

Come on!

Whatever light Arach had seen inside me needed to get to work. I had to find this lake, and my new power could come in real handy for that. I gave it my all, focusing every bit of energy I had on my magic.

Briefly, it flared to life, but it didn't tell me anything. I was hoping it would turn out to be like the FireSoul power, where they could ask it to help them find stuff and it would.

That didn't seem to be the case.

"Since it's not back here, let's try the other side of the house."

"Let's go, then."

We left the cellar and crept along the side of the building. It was quieter over here since we were down by the working part of the winery and it was night time. There was no gate to get out of the walls, though, so we had to go around the side.

The Cats of Catastrophe had disappeared somewhere, but maybe it was better that way. I wasn't sure that one or more of them wasn't a bit drunk off the wine. I drew another dagger as we snuck toward the corner of the house.

The night was silent, just a ripple of breeze, but it made the hair on my arms stand up. There had to be a lot of guards at a place like this.

No sooner had I thought it than one of them stepped out from behind the corner of the house. My heart jumped in my throat. He turned, eyes widening. We were so close that I could see his pupils and smell the rank scent of his dark magic.

I raised my dagger, but Connor was faster.

He punched him right in the nose. The demon reeled, and I struck, stabbing him in the heart with my blade. Connor punched him again, just to make sure he didn't scream. Or maybe he was just pissed about the whole captivity thing.

The demon crashed hard to his back, twitched, and then lay still.

"Good teamwork," Connor said.

"Yeah, I'll fight with you any day."

I knelt briefly to check his pockets, hoping for a cool weapon or maybe a transport charm. I came up empty, so I stood, eyeing the side of the house and the wall that was about twenty yards away. A guard sat on the ground next to a small but strong-looking gate, fast asleep.

He hadn't even noticed the commotion as we'd killed the other one.

"The lake probably isn't within the walls, is it?" I asked.

"Unlikely. This place is big, but that would make it crazy huge."

"Let's run for the gate, then. Maybe that guard will have a key."

"I like it. On three?"

"Just a moment." I drew a dagger from the ether. I got the sleeping guard in my sights and threw the blade. It pierced him in the neck, as expected. "Now you can count."

He grinned and counted up, and we ran, sprinting across the

grass. My lungs and muscles burned in tandem, and I prayed that no one was looking into the fields at this hour.

We reached the demon guard, who was already dead and starting to disappear to the underworld, and I patted him down for a key, finally finding one in his chest pocket. Muffin and his gang were nowhere to be seen, so this was lucky.

Quickly, I shoved the key into the lock, and we slipped out through the heavy iron gate. Then we started running again, racing to reach the woods that were about a hundred yards away.

I sprinted across the vineyards, running between twisted rows of dormant vine. By the time I stumbled into the shelter of the trees, I felt like I was about to pass out.

I propped my hands on my knees, panting.

Connor grabbed my arm. "Come on. Guards patrol these woods."

"Don't I know it." I gasped raggedly. I straightened and we set off, keeping to the shadows of the trees as we made our way to the front of the house.

The lake that glittered there made me want to fist pump. It was nestled in a valley below, pressed up against the woods. We'd have a bit of cover all the way there.

As we neared the lake, the sense of dark magic grew. It stank like a wet buffalo who'd been dancing with rotten eggs.

"We're close," I muttered. "But where is this Creeper's lair?"

"Under the lake, I think."

I swiveled to look at him. "*Under?*"

14

"Yeah, under the lake. Creepy, right?" He grinned.

"Totally." I inspected the lake shore, looking for some kind of passageway. All of the ground was undisturbed, though, revealing no clue of a trail leading to an entrance.

So I followed the dark magic, going to where the scent was the strongest. There was one section where it was even a bit hard to breathe. The ground was undisturbed, but there were a number of flat rocks clustered around the edge of the lake.

On a hunch, I began to step on them. Connor looked at me quizzically for a moment, then joined me.

When I stepped on a rock that depressed beneath my foot, I grinned. Magic swirled on the air, a faint sparkling feeling against my skin, and the ground gave way in front of me.

A hole opened up, the dirt parting to reveal a rustic stone staircase leading into the earth.

"Nice," Connor said.

I drew my sword from the ether and handed it to Connor. "Know how to use one of these?"

"I'm not bad." He took the sword.

I drew two daggers, then descended the steps, raising my

lightstone ring so that I could see what lay ahead. The stairs descended about two stories underground, leading to a passage that went straight toward the lake. It was made of stone and packed dirt, all of which was a bit wet. Everything smelled of damp earth.

I swiped my finger against the slimy wall to my right. "Does this feel like a death wish?"

"Yes."

In silence, we crept forward. With every step, I prayed that the lake wouldn't burst through these crappy walls and take us out.

As we walked, magic began to prickle more strongly against my skin. The farther we went, the worse it hurt.

"Feels like ant bites," Connor said.

"The Creeper clearly doesn't want visitors." I gripped my daggers, searching the passage ahead of us. Light gleamed at the end, green and sickly looking.

We crept forward, our footsteps silent. We were almost to the glowing green light when a massive spider lunged into the passage.

My lungs seized as fear chilled my skin.

The beast was the size of a small car, with fangs as long as my arm. Multifaceted eyes glared at us, and the thing charged forward. I threw my dagger right at one of its glittering eyes.

The dagger bounced off.

"What the heck!"

Connor charged past me, sword in hand. He dodged the striking spider's fangs and sliced at one of the legs. The limb fell off and exploded in a poof of black smoke.

I hurled my dagger at the spider's face, avoiding the eyes. The blade plunged into the middle of the monster's head, but it kept moving, darting for Connor as he danced around with the blade, going for the legs.

But the one he'd sliced off had already grown back.

He sliced off another, and it, too, began to regenerate. I raced toward them, calling on two more daggers. Two of my longest ones. It was a shame I didn't have two swords.

I crouched low to peer under the spider, and caught sight of a man with scraggly black and white hair standing in the room beyond. He seemed to be dancing in the middle of the cave-like room ahead of us.

Yeah, he *had* to be the Creeper. The name just fit too well.

As he danced, the spider struck out. Connor dived under the belly, so the spider came for me. I jumped left, avoiding the sharp fangs. Raw horror opened up inside of me at the sight of its mouth so close to my head.

I sliced at a leg with my dagger, trying to distract it while I figured out what the heck was going on and how we'd kill the thing. It was made of magic, clearly. The poofs of black smoke made that obvious.

But how could we destroy it when a dagger to the brain wouldn't do the job?

As I dodged the spider's blows, Connor attacked from the side.

I stole another glance at the man called the Creeper. He kept dancing, making strange movements with his arms and legs.

He actually kind of looked like a spider himself.

A pale white stone glowed around his neck.

The spider struck again. I dived low, sneaking under the belly and praying he wouldn't sit on me. As I slid beneath the spider, I caught sight of a glowing white stone set into the beast's belly.

Just like the one around the Creeper's neck.

Oh crap!

He was controlling the spider. And the stones linked them.

I dived back underneath the spider and stabbed up with my

blade. It pierced the glass crystal, and the beast exploded in a poof of powdery black ash.

"Whoa!" Connor cried. "Well done!"

"Thanks." I scrambled upright, spitting out the black powder and whirling to face the Creeper.

Connor and I stood at the entrance to the room. The Creeper stood in the middle, just twenty feet away. Rage lit his face. All around him, the cave-like room glowed an acid green. It looked like a mad scientist's lair, full of tables and shelves that were packed with magical tools and potions. A massive cauldron sat at the back, over which a glowing crystal was suspended. Blue smoke twined around the crystal.

Connor nodded at it. "That's the spell."

"Do you think you can figure out how to stop it while I hold him off?" I whispered. He was the potion master; I was the fighter. It only made sense.

"I'm on it." He started to inch toward the cauldron.

"I'll cover you." I lunged toward the Creeper, hurling a dagger right at him.

He dodged, fast as a snake, and threw a potion bomb at me. The red glass ball hurtled through the air, and I dived to the right, sliding across the floor. The bomb smashed into the stone and dirt wall behind me, exploding. Dirt and rocks flew outward, and I peered back to see a giant hole.

Crap!

That was one of the strongest explosive potions I'd ever seen.

I scrambled upright, calling on another dagger. I threw it, aiming for the chest, the biggest target. He was too fast for anything else.

He scuttled left, just like the spider we'd destroyed, and my dagger flew past.

How the heck was he so fast?

He grabbed another potion bomb off a table and flung it

toward me. I dived behind a wooden table. The bomb hit the right corner of it, and the thing lit on fire. The various potions on top began to pop and explode, sending off sparks of all different colors.

One emitted a huge blast of wind that blew me into the wall. Pain flared in my back as I slammed into a stone. The sound of a roaring storm filled the room, making my head pound. The noise was so loud that it became hard to think. It came from one of the potions that had been destroyed. A herd of white antelope exploded from another potion and leapt off the burning table. They stampeded around the room, then galloped through the tunnel, heading for the exit.

What the heck had been *in* some of those potions?

Through the chaos, I could see Connor racing around, grabbing vials off the tables and pouring them into the massive cauldron under the crystal. The smoke turned from blue to red. I had to guess that he recognized the spell and was trying to counteract it or something.

Thank fates he was here, because I'd have had no idea.

The Creeper was in the middle of the room, freaking out. He pulled at his hair as he turned his attention from me to Connor.

"Stop!" he shrieked. "You'll ruin it all!"

"That's the point!" Connor yelled. He tossed vials of potion into the cauldron.

The Creeper grabbed a red glass potion bomb off a table. *Red.*

That was the same one that had exploded the whole wall behind me. If it hit Connor, he'd be dead as a doornail.

I called a dagger from the ether and hurled it at the Creeper's back. This time, he couldn't see it to dodge. The blade sank into his shoulder, and he screamed, falling forward. His potion bomb exploded against the ground, blowing up in a massive cloud of smoke and debris.

Red debris.

The remains of the Creeper.

I cringed backward, gagging.

"Connor, are you okay?" I shouted as the smoke dissipated.

"Almost done!"

The smoke cleared enough that I spotted him chucking two more potion bombs into the cauldron. It began to boil and fizz, and Connor sprinted around it, racing for me.

The bubbles shot upward, surrounding the crystal that hung over it. When they splashed back down, the crystal was gone, devoured.

Strength and power flowed through my veins, feeling like an intravenous shot of magical espresso.

I gasped. "Whoa."

"Did it work?" Connor asked.

"I think so." I flung out my hands, envisioning my usual pale white shield. The shield burst forth, strong and true. "It worked!"

"Good. Because we're in trouble." He pointed toward the ceiling.

I dragged my gaze from the white shield and looked upward. All of the explosions had made an impact. The ceiling had begun to pour water through a crack.

The lake was breaking through.

"Run!" I turned and sprinted from the room, Connor at my side.

Behind us, a great crack and splash sounded. I looked back. The ceiling had fallen away, and water was pouring into the room. It rushed toward us. I sprinted harder, but soon it was lapping at my boots.

Panic clawed at my throat. We were only halfway through the tunnel. The water was to my knees. Running became a slog.

We sprinted harder but slower. Connor grabbed my hand, and we pulled each other along.

The water was to my thighs. It felt like running through pudding. Fear chilled my skin.

"We're almost there," Connor said.

Lungs and muscles burning, I gave it one last burst of speed and climbed onto the stairs. We raced up, leaving the flooding cave behind, and spilled out into the dark night.

I turned around, expecting the lake to be in turmoil. There was a slight ripple on the surface, but nothing more.

Panting, we raced deeper into the forest, taking cover in the trees.

I turned to Connor. "I think we did it."

"Your magic is back?"

"It is, and I bet my sisters have—"

"Ana?" Bree's voice whispered out of my comms charm. "Our magic is back."

"Yes!" Connor fist pumped.

"Where are you?" I asked.

"We've just arrived in the woods to the east of the house. We can see it."

"Perfect. Wait for us. We'll come find you."

Connor and I raced through the forest as silently as we could. Magic flowed through my veins, making me feel complete again.

"How did you know how to stop the curse?" I asked.

"I didn't. The potion in the cauldron was fueling the curse, which was trapped in the crystal hanging above. So I just decided to screw it up."

"Like a cake recipe?"

"Exactly."

At the edge of the forest, I spotted our backup. Lachlan caught my eye first, and something in my chest fluttered. I didn't want to call it butterflies, but yeah, it was definitely something like that.

Bree stood next to Cade and Rowan, and at her side stood Caro and Haris. Ali must have been recovering from his wounds. Everyone looked a bit beaten-up and tired, but I was so glad to see them.

Bree and Rowan threw their arms around me, then drew back and scowled.

Lachlan greeted Connor with a manly hug. The kind with back slapping that men seemed so fond of.

"I'm sorry," Lachlan said.

"Don't worry about it." Connor nodded. "I'm responsible for myself."

"That was so stupid," Rowan scolded me. "Going through an unknown portal!"

"It worked, didn't it?" I met Lachlan's gaze. He was standing close, his eyes glued to mine.

"Are you all right?" His voice was slightly rough. Worried. Tension stretched between us like a wire. The memory of the kiss flashed in my mind, but I banished it.

"Fine."

He nodded, then backed up, clearly trying to maintain the professional distance he'd insisted on.

I turned to Connor. "Do you have any idea where we might find the spell that they stole?"

"Not a clue," he said. "I can only guess that it's with their leader, and when they talk about him, they always refer to a garden."

"A garden?" Lachlan asked.

"Yes," said Connor. "But I've no idea why."

"Hmmm." I thought about the Creeper in his hidden lair beneath the lake. "Maybe it's supposed to be hidden and protected. Better than staying in the big house. That's an obvious target."

"True," Lachlan said. "Let's go find this garden."

We were about to leave the protection of the trees when a whisper came from behind us. "Connor."

A figure hurtled out of the trees, running on silent feet. She had dark hair and wore the leather clothing that was favored by mercenaries. A sword in a holster across her back completed the look, and a large bag hung at her side.

Claire, Connor's sister.

She hugged her brother hard as three others stepped out of the woods.

The FireSouls.

I grinned at Del, Nix, and Cass. "Perfect timing."

"Are we in time for a fight?" Cass asked, her red hair gleaming in the light of the moon. She wore a brown leather jacket and had two daggers strapped to her thighs. She was a FireSoul and a Mirror Mage, able to mimic anyone else's magic for a short while.

At her side stood Del, a half-Phantom FireSoul with black hair and clever blue eyes. She was dressed entirely in black leather. Nix, the third FireSoul, was a conjurer. Her cartoon cat T-shirt was at odds with her tough demeanor.

We'd helped them in fights in the past, and they'd never hesitated to return the favor.

"Yep, a big one," I said. "We're going to try to retrieve the *ancientus* spell."

"Ah, right." Understanding flicked in Nix's eyes as she looked at Lachlan.

Del nodded. "Well, seeing as we've finished with our other emergency task—because you found him—we're happy to help."

"We'll be backup," Cass said.

"Anything for the people who saved my brother," Claire added. She was a Fire Mage and mercenary, the closest friend of the FireSouls trio.

Heck yeah. With these four as backup, our odds of success had just doubled.

Claire handed her brother the sack that hung around her body. "Your potion bombs, brother dear. I thought we might need to fight our way out if we found you."

"Thanks, sis. You know the way to my heart." He handed me the sword I'd loaned him back in the Creeper's lair and patted the bag. "I've got my weapons of choice now."

"Thanks." I took the sword, then updated the newcomers on our plan to find and storm the garden, then turned to Bree. "Can you use your illusion to conceal us?"

"Partial invisibility, coming right up." She grinned. "Just enough to keep others from spotting us, but if we stick close, we'll be able to see each other. Barely."

"I'll dampen our sound," Lachlan said.

"Perfect," I said. "We'll head for the garden."

Bree's magic swelled on the air, and my friends disappeared. I squinted, just barely able to make out their outlines.

We set off at a jog across the vineyards, running up the rows of dormant vines toward the walled compound on the hill. Luck was with us, because there was no guard at the little gate. I turned the key, and we slipped inside, one by one.

I remembered seeing part of an amazing garden as I'd been carried in over the demon's shoulder. So I turned that way, whispering for my friends to follow.

They did, and we moved quickly alongside the outer edge of the house. A demon walked by, then stopped. He peered hard in our direction. Tension tightened my muscles, but he just shook his head as if he were seeing things and kept walking.

I grinned and kept going. We turned the corner of the house, and the familiar garden caught my eye. In the distance, a row of hedges stood. They looked merely decorative, but I doubted it.

We were close.

Then the hounds appeared.

Oh, crap.

Six of them stood in front of us. They were the size of large dogs, and each was covered in scales.

"Bad news," Bree muttered next to me.

The hounds looked toward us, confusion in their dark eyes. Around me, the faint outlines of my friends disappeared. Bree was upping her magic, making us fully invisible. I couldn't hear a single breath or rustle of grass beneath anyone's feet, so Lachlan had our sound completely dampened.

Then the hounds sniffed the air, their nostrils twitching.

Dread slipped like ice through my veins.

As one, the hounds lifted their heads and howled, their loud cries echoing in the night.

Demons burst out of the house to our right, spilling from three different doors. The hounds ran for us, circling our group. Helping the demons find us.

There had to be two dozen of them, all different species. Burnished red skin, gray, pale white, and dark green. Many were draped with weapons, but others were empty-handed, clearly planning to use just their magic. We were still fifty yards from the hedges.

"Drop the illusion, Bree!" I cried. We'd have to fight, and we didn't need to hit each other by mistake.

I didn't know if she could hear me through Lachlan's silence charm or if she just had the same idea as I did, but we all appeared.

The demons charged. So did we.

Caro, the Water Mage, shot a jet of water straight at the

closest demon. It plowed through his chest, shooting out the other side as a pink stream of blood-tinged water.

Haris did his usual, sprinting for a demon. A half second before he reached him, he turned invisible. Then the demon jerked upright and turned around, raising his hand and shooting a fireball at another demon. Haris would keep it up until his host was almost dead, then he'd jump out.

To my right, Lachlan shifted into his lion form. His black fur and mane gleamed in the light of the moon, and his roar shook the insides of my chest. He leapt toward a crowd of demons and tore off the head of the largest one. Blood sprayed, a violent display in the moonlight.

Rowan fought with her sword, fast as a burst of wind, while Bree struck down a demon with lightning.

Nix conjured a small fort made of sandbags. From their protective covering, Cass and Claire shot blasts of flame at the demons, taking them out one by one. Connor stood at their side, hurling his potion bombs with deadly accuracy. Del transformed into her Phantom self, a pale blue apparition that fought with a sword. Nothing could hurt her in that form, and she raced through the crowd of demons, dealing blows wherever she could.

But there are just so many of them.

More poured out of the house, heading straight for our group.

I flung a dagger into the chest of a nearby demon who blocked my path toward the garden. It pierced his heart, and he fell backward, arms whirling.

The battle raged all around as I fought my way toward the garden, Bree and Rowan at my side.

It was slow going, and no matter how many demons we killed, more appeared. Whoever owned this place was armed to the max. They purposely blocked my way to the garden, which only fueled me more.

The spell is in there.

Cass caught my eye. "Go! We'll cover you."

She and Claire began to shoot fireballs right into the crowd of demons who blocked our way.

It lightened the crowd, but it was still fierce.

There had to be twenty between us and the entrance between the hedges. It seemed impossible to get through.

Until Lachlan appeared at my side and knelt low on his front legs. The message was clear.

Get on.

Whoa. That was really personal. After our kiss, it'd be insanely personal.

But we needed to recover the *ancientus* spell before it could be used to bring back terrible magic from the past. And I'd be lying if I said I didn't want to climb on.

I climbed onto his back, almost immediately overwhelmed by the sense of *him*. Strength and honor and determination and fury.

He was enraged by what was happening, determined to do anything it took to make it right.

My heart thundered at the connection between us, at the raw ferocity of him.

Lachlan took off, bowling through the crowd of demons. I clung to his back, crouching low. Ahead of us, lightning struck as Bree took out some of the demons. Others fell to fire blasts and Connor's potion bombs.

Bree and Rowan raced after us.

A demon with long claws swiped at me, raking his claws across my arm as we ran by. Pain flared and blood flowed. I clung harder to Lachlan, wind tearing at my hair.

We plowed through the demons, and I leaned out with my

sword, taking the head off one. Another reached for me, claws glinting in the moonlight, but I took off his arm.

Finally, we reached the entrance between the hedgerow walls. I looked behind, just briefly, catching sight of the Fire-Souls, Claire, Connor, Caro, and Haris holding off the rest of the demons.

We wouldn't have stood a chance without them. But there was more ahead.

I turned to face what was coming.

15

The garden was quiet inside. Though a few demons tried to follow us in, our friends on the outside picked them off with fire and potion bombs.

Lachlan slowed his sprint as I clung to his back, muscles aching from desperately trying to hold on. Bree and Rowan caught up, slowing to a walk as they caught their breath. The four of us passed through multiple rows of hedges.

"This place is way bigger than it looks on the outside, isn't it?" Bree asked.

"Definitely," I said.

Beneath me, Lachlan rumbled his agreement. He moved with leonine grace, stalking toward the topiaries.

Should I get off of him?

I didn't really want to. This was fun.

"And we're onto something," Rowan said.

We passed another row of hedges, finally reaching a corridor lined on either side with topiaries. Animals of all different varieties bordered the path.

I inspected the topiaries, spotting giant monsters of all sorts.

Snakes, tigers, griffons, and demon dogs. They prowled and pranced, frozen in time.

As soon as we passed the first topiary, it burst to life. The cobra leapt off the platform, rearing its hooded head back to strike at Bree.

She called on her magic, and lightning struck, piercing the night sky and obliterating the topiary. It burnt to a crisp, ashes scattering to the ground.

The rest of the animals leapt to the ground, prowling near. I called on my sword, drawing it from the ether, and leapt off of Lachlan's back. For this, we were better separate.

He charged a panther topiary, while I raced for a bear. I struck out with my sword, doing a bit of gardening around the head. I sliced it right off. Headless, the bear swiped out with its front foot, swiping me across the stomach with its claws made of thorns.

Pain flared, and I doubled over briefly.

Keep fighting.

The wound wouldn't kill me—it would just hurt like hell. I straightened, aiming my sword for the bear's front leg. I lopped it off, then went for the next.

At my side, Rowan fought a stag. The antlers swiped out at her, coated with thorns.

I finished off the bear just as a shriek sounded. The Cats of Catastrophe appeared, racing toward the topiary beasts. They each leapt on their own monster, claws flailing. Snippets of leaves flew left and right as the cats each destroyed a topiary.

Lachlan cut through others, making quick work, while my sisters and I fought our way past three identical topiary alligators. Their tails whipped out with incredible strength. One knocked me off my feet, and I rolled out of the way of its snapping jaws. My hip ached where the gator's thorny tail had hit me, and blood soaked my jeans.

I turned and lunged, sword outstretched, and took off the monster's head.

Finally, we destroyed the last of the topiaries.

In the quiet calm, I surveyed what was ahead. About fifty yards away, a large stone building sat in the middle of a beautiful rose garden. Dark magic rolled out from the structure.

Our targets were in there. "Jackpot."

We stalked closer on silent feet, keeping our pace quick. We'd only gone about ten yards when dark figures melted out from the walls, stalking toward us. They had gray skin and black eyes, with long pointed ears close to their skulls. Black claws tipped their hands. Their auras were as black as pitch, swirling around them like fog. Pale yellow eyes gleamed at us as they licked their fangs.

"Dark fae." Fear echoed in Rowan's voice.

The Cats of Catastrophe hissed and ran backward, putting distance between themselves and the creatures.

Cold shivered across my skin.

The dark fae's touch was deadly. And they were super fast.

They streaked toward us. My heart leapt into my throat as I threw up my arms, creating a massive white shield. They slammed into it, hissing and clawing.

There were at least twenty of them. They were so fast and so deadly that we couldn't fight them. Not all of them.

"Shit, what do we do?" Bree asked. "I can electrocute some, but how long can you hold that shield?"

Sweat broke out on my brow, and my arms shook. "Not long."

Next to me, Lachlan shifted back into his human form and raised his arms.

"Hurry." I gasped as my shield began to flicker. Whatever he was going to do, he needed to do it quick.

The dark fae were so strong that they were breaking down

my shield. They'd overwhelm us in seconds. Fear like I'd never known shivered through me, turning all my muscles to ice.

I could take out one or two, and my sisters probably more. But not enough. At least one could touch us, poisoning us with a fast-acting dose of lethal paralysis. For this, they were one of the most feared species of magical creature.

Lachlan raised his hands. His magic surged. Behind the dark fae, the earth rose up. A wall of dirt and rocks cut off our view of the stone building as it curled over the fae like a tidal wave. It crashed down on them, dirt and rocks pouring down, crushing them.

Shocked, I stared. All I could see was piles of displaced dirt and stone. The fae were pulverized beneath.

"Come on!" Lachlan started to climb over the piles of dirt and rock.

I followed. "How the hell did you do that?"

It must have taken *so* much magic.

"Practice." His voice sounded a bit strange. "And I'm nearly tapped out. It took almost everything I have."

"So we're on our own in there." I pointed to the building, which was only ten yards away now.

"I can still fight. Maybe even shift."

We reached the building and rushed inside, Lachlan taking the lead.

The interior was far larger than I'd expected. Shelves of books and scrolls bordered the walls, along with massive iron safes full of who knew what. Tables were scattered here and there with papers spread about. Maps and documents.

But it was the people in the middle who caught my eye.

Our targets.

And they were ready for us.

The cloaked figure and the two women from the Roman baths stood there. The dark-haired woman and the blonde one had brought him the spell and hadn't left his side, it seemed. His minions. They were guarded by two hulking demons who each held massive swords. The cloaked figure's magic rolled out, dark and fierce. It made my stomach turn and my muscles tremble. In his hands, he clutched the package with the spell.

In front of them, two demons struggled with something on the ground. They pulled a big iron ring—just like the trapdoor in the ghost library.

We stepped forward.

Thunder cracked. The roof shook.

Bree was trying to break through with her lightning, but the building was strong.

The women at the cloaked figure's side stepped forward. The dark-haired one hurled a blast of green magic at us.

Crap!

This was the same combustive magic that she'd thrown back at the Roman baths. I dived left, narrowly avoiding a kill shot. The edges of the magic hit my arm, making it go limp as I crashed to the ground. The blast of magic destroyed the wall behind me.

Pain surged through my arm as I scrambled to my feet. The limb hung limply at my side, impossible to move.

Rowan sprinted for the woman, sword raised. The blonde woman hurled a massive icicle at Rowan, who dodged the thing by inches.

Bree fought the two demons, using her wings to fly just out of their reach as she delivered killing blows.

The cloaked figure raised his hands. Foul magic swelled on the air. Wispy black figures shot from his fingertips, rushing toward us. There were at least fifteen of them, and all looked like shadowy grim reapers.

They converged on us, bringing with them the stink of death.

I called upon my magic, dredging up every bit of it, and envisioned my shield. The light burst out of me, but it wasn't my shield at all. It was a pale glow that felt like a summer day.

What the heck?

Use it.

Fear clawed at my throat. This wasn't my shield. It couldn't protect us.

Give it your life force.

I had no idea what that meant.

Try.

Crap, this was new magic. And it wanted me to do something totally confusing. I tried, focusing on the commands, pushing my energy into the magic, making it glow brighter and stronger.

The grim reaper figures shrank away from the light. I could almost feel the rage and confusion flowing from the cloaked figure. Sweat dripped down my face as I worked, pushing all the energy in my body out through my hands.

On instinct, I started calling up good memories. My mother from when I was younger. Playing with my sisters. A single trip to the beach when our lives were still easy.

The light glowed stronger, making the evil shadows begin to fade. But weakness stole over me. As I fed my energy to the magic, it became harder to stand. Harder to breathe.

At my side, Lachlan shifted into his lion form, no doubt using the last of his magic. He roared, and charged the cloaked figure. The women were on either side of the room already, battling Bree and Rowan.

I kept up my strange new magic, beating back the shadowy figures who still threatened to overwhelm us.

Just before Lachlan collided with the cloaked man, he hurled the package containing the spell at the blonde woman. She was about to catch it when Muffin leapt into the air and batted it away. He must have charged into the building.

The package with the crystal flew to the side of the room.

Lachlan collided with the cloaked figure, taking him down to the ground. In a burst of strength, the cloaked figure shoved the lion off of him. Lachlan flew through the air and slammed to the ground on the other side of the room.

Holy crap!

Whoever wore the cloak was really freaking strong. In front of him, the demons finally managed to pull the trapdoor open.

My muscles were trembling with strain as I fought back the shadowy forms with my magic. I was nearly tapped out, ready to fall on my face, but I kept going.

There was no other choice.

The cloaked man rose to his feet and surveyed the room. Rowan was on the left, plunging her blade into the stomach of the dark-haired woman. Bree, who had finished off the demons, was now taking out the blonde. Lachlan rose to his feet and charged him again. The dark shadows—his creepy army—were almost gone.

Frustration vibrated from the cloaked figure.

He was losing.

And he knew it.

He flung out his hands and hurled jets of green fire into the room, then he jumped into the trapdoor below.

Primordial fire!

My throat closed with fear.

This kind of fire could devour this building in seconds.

"Run!" Bree screamed.

She abandoned her fight with the woman at the back of the room and sprinted toward me. As the green flames devoured the walls, Lachlan hurtled our way, and Muffin ran so fast he was a blur.

The demons who'd opened the trapdoor didn't bother to jump in; they just turned and ran for the door.

As Bree passed by the trapdoor, she glanced inside, then screamed, "Full of fire!"

The fire had already devoured the part of the room where the crystal containing the spell had landed.

Screw that.

I turned and ran, sprinting alongside my friends. The space was nearly full of green flame, the heat so great that I could smell burning hair. I raced through the door with my sisters, spilling out into the cool night.

We kept running, following Muffin into the garden. Lachlan ran behind us, alongside the demons. They veered off to the left, but we ignored them, wanting to put more space between us and the building.

We didn't stop until we were fifty yards away. Panting, I turned. The building was a giant green torch. Even the stone was on fire.

"The spell is destroyed," Rowan said. "And the blonde woman didn't make it out."

Muffin meowed. *You're welcome.*

"Good job, bud." I looked at Lachlan, who stood next to me in his lion form. He was enormous, his black fur glinting in the light. Nerves skated across my skin as my gaze traveled from his fangs to claws, though I knew he'd never hurt me.

I squinted at one of the long claws on his front right foot. The deadly claw pierced a tiny scrap of brown cloth. *Just like what the cloaked figure had worn.* I gasped, then bent and pulled it off the claw. I shoved it in my pocket.

Lachlan shifted back to human. "Where did he go? That trapdoor had to lead somewhere."

"He filled it with flame to cover his tracks," Bree said. "It looked like the pits of hell when I passed."

"I think it must go to the portal in the woods," I said. "I bet that was his escape hatch to get there."

"Let's try to catch him."

"I'll fly." Bree's wings unfurled, silver and bright. She shot into the air, flying up over the forest.

Lachlan met my gaze. "Want to come?"

He was fastest in his lion form, which meant....

"Yes."

Magic swirled around him as he shifted. Then the enormous beast stood in front of me, regal and terrifying. I stashed my sword in the ether and climbed onto his back, clinging to his warm fur. My wounded arm hung limp at my side, making it difficult, so I clutched him with my knees.

"I'll alert our friends," Rowan said.

Muffin stood by her side, whiskers singed. Princess Snowflake III and Bojangles had appeared as well. As usual, Princess Snowflake III was coated liberally in blood, while Bojangles just looked like Bojangles. Messy fur and goofy grin.

"Be safe," I said to Rowan, right before Lachlan started sprinting through the garden.

In the courtyard, he raced past my friends, who were finishing off the last of the demons. They looked battered and worn, but no one was on the ground, at least.

I crouched low over Lachlan's back, clinging tight to his fur as the wind tore at my hair.

Come on. Come on.

We had to beat the figure to the portal.

Lachlan sprinted through the small gate.

"Across the vineyard, to the forest!" I screamed.

Lachlan hadn't arrived using that portal—only I had. Bree had a bird's-eye view from the sky, but Lachlan needed directions. He cut through the rows of dormant vines, then sprinted into the forest. Branches tore at my clothes and hair as we ran. I yelled directions, trying to remember which way I'd come initially.

Then we saw it—the stone ruins where the portal gleamed with golden light. It glowed in the distance.

"You see that?" Bree's voice sounded through my comms charm. "It just lit up. I'm going in."

Lachlan picked up the pace, his giant strides eating up the ground. As we neared, I spotted someone standing within the glowing light. The cloaked figure.

Bree hurtled from the sky, her silver wings carrying her down.

The light around the figure shined brighter. We were almost there!

Then he disappeared. The light went black.

Lachlan sprinted into the stone ruins, but they lay dormant and quiet. The tumbled columns gleamed in the moonlight, but there was no more magic here.

He was gone.

16

The next day, I stood outside Arach's office, waiting to be called in. My wounded arm was in a sling, still aching. Whatever that woman had hit me with had done some real damage. Hedy, who acted as the healer as well as inventor, had patched me up some, but it'd take a couple days to fully heal.

Both women had died in the fire, so I'd come out on the better end in that scenario, at least.

I tapped my foot, studying the stone wall in front of me. Worry ate at my mind, making me jittery.

Finally, the door creaked open. Jude gestured me inside. Arach stood at the head of the table, her silvery form glimmering in the light.

As usual, her power rolled over me, crashing and pulling like waves. She gestured to a chair. "You can take a seat."

I did, fidgeting with my good hand.

"You did well," Arach said. "Jude has told me what happened in Tuscany, and it sounds like you saved the day."

Warmth flowed through me, followed by a tug of concern. "We didn't save the spell, though. And whoever was behind the theft got away."

"The spell was destroyed," Jude said. "So that's the same difference. As long as it can't be used by the wrong people, we count it as a success. As for the mastermind, we'll catch him. But you came out on top, Ana. Lachlan has deposited the reward money in your account."

The wind rushed out of my lungs. "Really?"

"Really. Without you, we may not have stopped the *ancientus* spell from being used for evil. And Connor could have died."

"Wow." I had no idea what to do with that kind of money. Save it, probably. Though it seemed like a lot, if I ever had to leave the Protectorate, I'd need it. But the most important question still remained. The thing that I *really* wanted. More than half a million pounds. More than almost anything. "How does this affect me at the academy? Can I advance to the next level?"

Jude nodded. "You've done well. Real-world scenarios are better for you than training exercises, it appears."

My shoulders relaxed, and I grinned. Thank fates. I couldn't keep spinning my wheels in class.

"You'll still have to do some exercises with your classmates, of course," Jude said. "But this went a long way."

Arach sat. "Jude is correct. You're proving yourself, Ana. Well done."

"Thanks." Worry tugged at me. "Do you have any idea what pantheon I might be? I have two new powers, but no idea who gave them to me." I hated the wondering.

"How would you describe the powers?" Arach leaned forward, interest gleaming in her eyes.

"I have one that is like prophecy—sort of. It helps me answer questions. And I have some kind of light that feeds on my energy but can repel darkness and sickness."

Arach's brows rose. "Interesting. Those sound unusual. But I have no idea what pantheon they could belong to."

"We don't have enough information," Jude said. "Until you know more about them, it's a mystery."

Damn.

"The light must be what helped you resist the dark curse that stole everyone else's magic," Arach said. "It's a magic that resists and survives. In the end, it's what helped you find the *ancientus* curse."

"You'll have to learn to use it," Jude said. "You'll need your magic to pass the academy."

"And to survive," Arach added. "Now that your magic is appearing, you're going to need to learn to harness it, or it will devour you."

I nodded, determined to succeed.

"We'll help you, Ana," Jude said. "But most of it will be up to you. Success or failure, life or death. It's all on your shoulders."

I nodded, swallowing hard.

I can do this.

I have to do this.

After the meeting, I hurried through the ancient, winding corridors up to my apartment. It was nearly seven, and the sun had long since set. I was supposed to meet our friends at the Whisky and Warlock to celebrate, and I was running late.

It'd been because I had a meeting with the most powerful figures at the Protectorate, but Bree and Rowan wouldn't take that excuse when they were ready to party.

Slightly out of breath, I let myself into my apartment. As usual, the Cats of Catastrophe lounged on the couch. A bowl of potato chips sat between them, but there were no people present.

I pointed. "Those yours?"

Bojangles snagged a chip out of the bowl and crunched down.

"I guess so." My gaze caught on the easel on the side wall. There was a new painting on it.

What the heck?

I stepped closer.

It was a painting of a dead mouse sitting on a doorstep. There was a red heart in the corner. It was a rough image, looking like it'd been done with fingerpaints.

"I did *not* paint that," I muttered as I turned to the cats. "Did you see who did this?"

Muffin and Bojangles both meowed. Princess Snowflake III just stared at me. My eyes flicked to her paw. Brown and red paint dotted her toes.

My eyes widened. "You?"

"Meow."

I looked back at the painting.

Holy crap, it was a gift.

Most cats brought their people dead rodents as a sign of affection. Or perhaps to feed their hapless and pathetic owners who couldn't hunt properly. Who really knew.

But *this* was definitely a present from Princess Snowflake III. She hadn't caught me a mouse. She'd painted me one.

I looked back at her, shocked. "So you *do* like me!"

She hissed.

I looked at Muffin. "Care to translate?"

She likes you.

"But the hissing?"

She's not eating your face, is she?

I grinned and looked at Princess Snowflake III. "I like you, too, Princess."

She hissed again.

"Excuse me. Princess Snowflake III."

She jumped off the couch, strolled up to me, and butted her head against my shin. Then she turned abruptly and returned to the couch, smearing a bit of red paint on the fabric.

I sighed, looking at my gruesome new painting. "I guess I'll have to hang it in the entranceway!"

An hour later, after they'd spent an appropriate amount of time oohing and aahing over my new painting, Bree and Rowan accompanied me to the Whisky and Warlock. It was our favorite place in Edinburgh. In fact, it was everyone's favorite place.

The Whisky and Warlock was the official pub of the Protectorate, and we had our own little room in the twisty and turny old place. Fortunately, it was just a short walk away, through the enchanted glen and the portal that took us directly to the Grassmarket.

The night was windy and cold as we walked down the cobblestone street to the pub. I pushed open the door and ducked under the low doorway, sighing at the warmth and the golden glow. The pub was like a maze, full of little rooms and nooks and crannies. I went left, into the little room where the Protectorate always gathered.

As I entered, everyone started clapping. Though some of my fellow students just stared at me, unimpressed.

Ha! Take that, Lavender and Angus.

I smiled. Normally, we celebrated our victories and mourned our defeats in this little room. But I'd never been the recipient of the applause before. It was kind of nice.

The fire crackled in the hearth, and the old wooden bar gleamed under the warm light. Muffin sat at a bar stool, and I had no idea how he'd gotten here faster than me. He had a martini glass full of cream in front of him and wore a new gemstone in his ear. Next to him sat Kitty, the plump black cat who lived here. Kitty was a girl as far as I knew, which meant that Muffin was on a date?

I stifled a chuckle and wished him luck. With his singed whiskers, he was going to have to be extra charming.

"Come on. Let's get drinks!" Bree said.

"Ana's paying!" Rowan crowed.

I grinned. I could spare some of my new nest egg, especially for these guys.

We squeezed up to the bar. Sophie, the bartender, had her dark hair pulled up. Today, her T-shirt read *Don't Mess With Nessie.* She grinned widely. "Glass of bubbly for you?"

"Please!" I grinned. "And a pink cocktail for Bree and whatever weird thing Rowan is drinking these days."

Rowan laughed and punched me lightly on the shoulder. We hopped up on the barstools, careful to give Muffin his space. Sophie delivered our drinks.

"You did good, Ana." Bree sipped her pink drink.

"Thanks." I leaned against her, happy. We chatted for a while, stopping occasionally to talk with the people who swung by. Caro, Ali, and Haris joined us, and we started up a game of pool in the back room.

As usual, Caro wiped the floor with us. She'd done a short stint as a pool shark a few years ago, and it showed. We played for a couple hours. Every thirty minutes or so, I'd look around for Lachlan, hoping to see him. But there was no reason for him to be at our hangout. I hadn't seen him since last night in the infirmary. He'd had more injuries than I'd realized—the cloaked figure had broken several of his ribs when he'd thrown him across the room.

Eventually, we headed home. It would be an early day of classes tomorrow. As we walked out of the pub, I craned my neck around, looking for him once more.

But nope. He was nowhere to be seen.

I frowned, disappointed, then followed my friends out. The wind was bitter as we made our way down the street and through the portal to the Protectorate. It was even colder in the Highlands, and we ran all the way back to the castle, jumping over gnarled old tree roots in the enchanted glen and sprinting across the great lawn.

I was gasping and laughing by the time we pushed through the doors, so grateful to have this as my home and my new life. It'd been hard on the outside. Hard and dangerous and scary.

Life could still be those things here, but we had backup. Support.

Grinning, I followed my friends across the entry hall.

"Ana." Lachlan's voice made me pull up short.

I turned. He stood at the entrance of the hallway that led to Arach's office.

"Ana?" Bree whispered.

"You can go." My heart was already racing. I approached him, completely ignoring my sister. Classy. "What's up?"

My heart was lodged in my chest. Could this be the last time I saw him?

"How do you feel?" he asked. Concern glinted in his eyes.

I shrugged with my good shoulder, regretting the move when it pulled on my injured arm. "Fine. It'll heal. You?"

"Much better."

A large crowd of laughing Protectorate members entered the hall, so we stepped into an alcove behind us. The crowd turned right, directly toward us. They piled into the hallway, forcing us deeper into the alcove, where the shadows lingered.

It pushed us closer together, and I couldn't help the shiver that raced through me. I searched Lachlan's gaze, hoping to see the same heat.

Maybe I did, or maybe it was wishful thinking. The flames were banked within his dark eyes.

"I wanted to thank you for your help," he said.

"Thanks for the opportunity. It was fun. And profitable." Oh fates. Was that weird? Should I have said that?

I gave a mental shrug. Not much I could do about it now! If I was going to feel weird about something, it should probably be the fact that I'd been sucking on his face a couple days ago. And the fact that he'd had to break the kiss and remind me that we were working together.

I blushed.

His gaze traced over my cheeks, which just made me realize that he *noticed* me blushing.

Perfect.

I was a badass who'd started driving across Death Valley when I was sixteen, and here I was, blushing.

"I wanted to make you an offer," he said.

"An offer?"

"I don't know what you are—you've been too cagey to share —but you have powerful magic. It was you that made the difference between failure and success on this mission. I want to find the cloaked figure, and I want you to help."

"Me?" *Okay, idiot. He already made that clear.*

"Aye, you." His lips curved up at the corners. "It will take time to find him—we have almost no clues. Just the scrap of fabric that my claw pulled off his cloak. Thank you for spotting that, by the way. We may be able to use it to track him. Eventually, we'll get a lead. When we do, I want your help."

"And I'd be working with you on this."

"Aye. We'll hunt him together. In return, I'll help you with your magic."

"How can you help me?"

"I wasn't born with twelve fully developed powers. They

were seeds of different gifts, only partially there. But with practice, they grew."

"I've never heard of that." Normally, you had what you had. It took some practice, sure, but no one ever described their magic as *partially there*. Also, no one had ever had twelve powers before.

"It's rare. But I can help you. And you can help me."

"Um." My mind raced. But what was I going to say? *No?* Heck no. "Yeah, I'll do it. I want to get that bastard. And the help sounds good." Fates knew I was a mess.

"And if we catch him, it will help you at the Academy. I can talk to Jude about it."

"That's just what I need." Outside jobs were easier for me than the academy for some reason, and I wanted to pass. This could help me do that. More than that, I wanted to spend time with Lachlan.

"But there's one thing." He looked vaguely uncomfortable.

"What is it?"

"The kiss."

My cheeks blazed, and I wanted to dunk my head in a bucket of freezing water. "What about it?"

"It shouldn't happen again. Not as long as we're working together on this."

"Uh." I swallowed hard. That wasn't really an official Protectorate rule. Some people liked to try to abide by it, but they didn't *have* to.

But Lachlan wanted to.

Which meant he didn't want to kiss me again.

And now I couldn't exactly say, "I've changed my mind. I won't help you hunt the bad guy because you won't kiss me."

Yeah, that wasn't an option.

Cheeks burning, I nodded. "Yeah, of course. Good idea. Fabulous."

Go on. Keep babbling. I forced myself to hold his gaze, unable to read what was in his eyes. Heat? Regret?

Maybe.

I wanted there to be.

But they were just professional. I remembered how intense the kiss was, but it seemed he might not.

Just my luck.

"Thank you, Ana." He squeezed my shoulder. It was clearly supposed to be a friendly gesture, but heat zinged down my arm.

From the way his eyes widened slightly and how he jerked his hand back, he felt the same.

There was an undeniable connection between us. A heat I'd never felt before.

And he was determined to ignore it.

"I'll see you soon," he said.

I nodded. "Yep. Later."

His gaze held mine for just a second more, then he turned and left. I watched him walk away, turning to peer around the corner of the alcove as he strode through the hall and out into the cold night.

Oh fates, what had I gotten myself into?

THANK YOU FOR READING!

I hope you enjoyed Ana's first book as much as I enjoyed writing it. Reviews are *so* helpful to authors. If you want to leave one, you can do so on Amazon.

Join my mailing list to stay updated. You'll also get a free copy of *Hidden Magic*, the story of the FireSouls' early adventures. Turn the page for an excerpt of *Hidden Magic*. The story stars Cass, the girl that Bree and Cade visited in Magic's Bend.

EXCERPT OF HIDDEN MAGIC

Jungle, Southeast Asia
   Five years before the events in Ancient Magic

"How much are we being paid for this job again?" I glanced at the dudes filling the bar. It was a motley crowd of supernaturals, many of whom looked shifty as hell.

"Not nearly enough for one as dangerous as this." Del frowned at the man across the bar, who was giving her his best sexy face. There was a lot of eyebrow movement happening. "Is he having a seizure?"

"Looks like it." Nix grinned. "Though I gotta say, I wasn't expecting this. We're basically in a tree, for magic's sake. In the middle of the jungle! Where are all these dudes coming from?"

"According to my info, there's a mining operation near here. Though I'd say we're more *under* a tree than *in* a tree."

"I'm with Cass," Del said. "Under, not in."

"Fair enough," Nix said.

We were deep in Southeast Asia, in a bar that had long ago been reclaimed by the jungle. A massive fig tree had grown over and around the ancient building, its huge roots strangling the stone walls. It was straight out of a fairy tale.

Monks had once lived here, but a few supernaturals of indeterminate species had gotten ahold of it and turned it into a watering hole for the local supernaturals. We were meeting our contact here, but he was late.

"Hey, pretty lady." A smarmy voice sounded from my left. "What are you?"

I turned to face the guy who was giving me the up and down, his gaze roving from my tank top to my shorts. He wasn't Clarence, our local contact. And if he meant "what kind of supernatural are you?" I sure as hell wouldn't be answering. That could get me killed.

"Not interested is what I am," I said.

"Aww, that's no way to treat a guy." He grabbed my hip, rubbed his thumb up and down.

I smacked his hand away, tempted to throat-punch him. It was my favorite move, but I didn't want to start a fight before Clarence got here. Didn't want to piss off our boss.

The man raised his hands. "Hey, hey. No need to get feisty. You three sisters?"

I glanced at Nix and Del, at their dark hair that was so different from my red. We were all about twenty, but we looked nothing alike. And while we might call ourselves sisters—*deirfiúr* in our native Irish—this idiot didn't know that.

"Go away." I had no patience for dirt bags who touched me without asking. "Run along and flirt with your hand, because that's all the action you'll be getting tonight."

His face turned a mottled red, and he raised a fist. His magic welled, the scent of rotten fruit overwhelming.

He thought he was going to smack me? Or use his magic against me?

Ha.

I lashed out, punching him in the throat. His eyes bulged and he gagged. I kneed him in the crotch, grinning when he keeled over.

"Hey!" A burly man with a beard lunged for us, his buddy beside him following. "That's no way—"

"To treat a guy?" I finished for him as I kicked out at him. My tall, heavy boots collided with his chest, sending him flying backward. I never used my magic—didn't want to go to jail and didn't want to blow things up—but I sure as hell could fight.

His friend raised his hand and sent a blast of wind at us. It threw me backward, sending me skidding across the floor.

By the time I'd scrambled to my feet, a brawl had broken out in the bar. Fists flew left and right, with a bit of magic thrown in. Nothing bad enough to ruin the bar, like jets of flame, because no one wanted to destroy the only watering hole for a hundred miles, but enough that it lit up the air with varying magical signatures.

Nix conjured a baseball bat and swung it at a burly guy who charged her, while Del teleported behind a horned demon and smashed a chair over his head. I'd always been jealous of Del's ability to sneak up on people like that.

All in all, it was turning into a good evening. A fight between supernaturals was fun.

"Enough!" the bartender bellowed. "Or no more beer!"

The patrons quieted immediately. Fights might be fun, but they weren't worth losing beer over.

I glared at the jerk who'd started it. There was no way I'd take the blame, even though I'd thrown the first punch. He should have known better.

The bartender gave me a look and I shrugged, hiking a thumb at the jerk who'd touched me. "He shoulda kept his hands to himself."

"Fair enough," the bartender said.

I nodded and turned to find Nix and Del. They'd grabbed our beers and were putting them on a table in the corner. I went to join them.

We were a team. Sisters by choice, ever since we'd woken in a field at fifteen with no memories other than those that said we were FireSouls on the run from someone who had hurt us. Who was hunting us.

Our biggest goal, even bigger than getting out from under our current boss's thumb, was to save enough money to buy concealment charms that would hide us from the monster who hunted us. He was just a shadowy memory, but it was enough to keep us running.

"Where is Clarence, anyway?" I pulled my damp tank top away from my sweaty skin. The jungle was damned hot. We couldn't break into the temple until Clarence gave us the information we needed to get past the guard at the front. And we didn't need to spend too much longer in this bar.

Del glanced at her watch, her blue eyes flashing with annoyance. "He's twenty minutes late. Old Man Bastard said he should be here at eight."

Old Man Bastard—OMB for short—was our boss. His name said it all. Del, Nix, and I were FireSouls, the most despised species of supernatural because we could steal other magical being's powers if we killed them. We'd never done that, of course, but OMB didn't care. He'd figured out our secret when we were too young to hide it effectively and had been blackmailing us to work for him ever since.

It'd been four years of finding and stealing treasure on his behalf. Treasure hunting was our other talent, a gift from the dragon with whom legend said we shared a soul. No one had seen a dragon in centuries, so I wasn't sure if the legend was even true, but dragons were covetous, so it made sense they had a knack for finding treasure.

"What are we after again?" Nix asked.

"A pair of obsidian daggers," Del said. "Nice ones."

"And how much is this job worth?" Nix repeated my earlier question. Money was always on our minds. It was our only chance at buying our freedom, but OMB didn't pay us enough for it to be feasible anytime soon. We kept meticulous track of our earnings and saved like misers anyway.

"A thousand each."

"Damn, that's pathetic." I slouched back in my chair and stared up at the ceiling, too bummed about our crappy pay to even be impressed by the stonework and vines above my head.

"Hey, pretty ladies." The oily voice made my skin crawl. We just couldn't get a break in here. I looked up to see Clarence, our contact.

Clarence was a tall man, slender as a vine, and had the slicked back hair and pencil-thin mustache of a 1940s movie star. Unfortunately, it didn't work on him. Probably because his stare was like a lizard's. He was more Gomez Addams than Clark Gable. I'd bet anything that he liked working for OMB.

"Hey, Clarence," I said. "Pull up a seat and tell us how to get into the temple."

Clarence slid into a chair, his movement eerily snakelike. I shivered and scooted my chair away, bumping into Del. The scent of her magic flared, a clean hit of fresh laundry, as she no doubt suppressed her instinct to transport away from Clarence. If I had her gift of teleportation, I'd have to repress it as well.

"How about a drink first?" Clarence said.

Del growled, but Nix interjected, her voice almost nice. She had the most self control out of the three of us. "No can do, Clarence. You know... Mr. Oribis"—her voice tripped on the name, probably because she wanted to call him OMB—"wants the daggers soon. Maybe next time, though."

"Next time." Clarence shook his head like he didn't believe

her. He might be a snake, but he was a clever one. His chest puffed up a bit. "You know I'm the only one who knows how to get into the temple. How to get into any of the places in this jungle."

"And we're so grateful you're meeting with us. Mr. Oribis is so grateful." Nix dug into her pocket and pulled out the crumpled envelope that contained Clarence's pay. We'd counted it and found—unsurprisingly—that it was more than ours combined, even though all he had to do was chat with us for two minutes. I'd wanted to scream when I'd seen it.

Clarence's gaze snapped to the money. "All right, all right."

Apparently his need to be flattered went out the window when cash was in front of his face. Couldn't blame him, though. I was the same way.

"So, what are we up against?" I asked.

The temple containing the daggers had been built by supernaturals over a thousand years ago. Like other temples of its kind, it was magically protected. Clarence's intel would save us a ton of time and damage to the temple if we could get around the enchantments rather than breaking through them.

"Dvarapala. A big one."

"A gatekeeper?" I'd seen one of the giant, stone monster statues at another temple before.

"Yep." He nodded slowly. "Impossible to get through. The temple's as big as the Titanic—hidden from humans, of course —but no one's been inside in centuries, they say."

Hidden from humans was a given. They had no idea supernaturals existed, and we wanted to keep it that way.

"So how'd you figure out the way in?" Del asked. "And why *haven't* you gone in? Bet there's lots of stuff you could fence in there. Temples are usually full of treasure."

"A bit of pertinent research told me how to get in. And I'd

rather sell the entrance information and save my hide. It won't be easy to get past the booby traps in there."

Hide? Snakeskin, more like. Though he had a point. I didn't think he'd last long trying to get through a temple on his own.

"So? Spill it," I said, anxious to get going.

He leaned in, and the overpowering scent of cologne and sweat hit me. I grimaced, held my breath, then leaned forward to hear his whispers.

As soon as Clarence walked away, the communications charms around my neck vibrated. I jumped, then groaned. Only one person had access to this charm.

I shoved the small package Clarence had given me into my short's pocket and pressed my fingertips to the comms charm, igniting its magic.

"Hello, Mr. Oribis." I swallowed my bile at having to be polite.

"Girls," he grumbled.

Nix made a gagging face. We hated when he called us girls.

"Change of plans. You need to go to the temple tonight."

"What? But it's dark. We're going tomorrow." He never changed the plans on us. This was weird.

"I need the daggers sooner. Go tonight."

My mind raced. "The jungle is more dangerous in the dark. We'll do it if you pay us more."

"Twice the usual," Del said.

A tinny laugh echoed from the charm. "Pay *you* more? You're lucky I pay you at all."

I gritted my teeth and said, "But we've been working for you for four years without a raise."

"And you'll be working for me for four more years. And four after that. And four after that." Annoyance lurked in his tone. So did his low opinion of us.

Del's and Nix's brows crinkled in distress. We'd always suspected that OMB wasn't planning to let us buy our freedom, but he'd dangled that carrot in front of us. What he'd just said made that seem like a big fat lie, though. One we could add to the many others he'd told us.

An urge to rebel, to stand up to the bully who controlled our lives, seethed in my chest.

"No," I said. "You treat us like crap, and I'm sick of it. Pay us fairly."

"I treat you like *crap,* as you so eloquently put it, because that is exactly what you are. *FireSouls.*" He spit the last word, imbuing it with so much venom I thought it might poison me.

I flinched, frantically glancing around to see if anyone in the bar had heard what he'd called us. Fortunately, they were all distracted. That didn't stop my heart from thundering in my ears as rage replaced the fear. I opened my mouth to shout at him, but snapped it shut. I was too afraid of pissing him off.

"Get it by dawn," he barked. "Or I'm turning one of you in to the Order of the Magica. Prison will be the least of your worries. They might just execute you."

I gasped. "You wouldn't." Our government hunted and imprisoned—or destroyed—FireSouls.

"Oh, I would. And I'd enjoy it. The three of you have been more trouble than you're worth. You're getting cocky, thinking you have a say in things like this. Get the daggers by dawn, or one of you ends up in the hands of the Order."

My skin chilled, and the floor felt like it had dropped out from under me. He was serious.

"Fine." I bit off the end of the word, barely keeping my voice from shaking. "We'll do it tonight. Del will transport them to you as soon as we have them."

"Excellent." Satisfaction rang in his tone, and my skin crawled. "Don't disappoint me, or you know what will happen."

The magic in the charm died. He'd broken the connection.

I collapsed back against the chair. In times like these, I wished I had it in me to kill. Sure, I offed demons when they came at me on our jobs, but that was easy because they didn't actually die. Killing their earthly bodies just sent them back to their hell.

But I couldn't kill another supernatural. Not even OMB. It might get us out of this lifetime of servitude, but I didn't have it in me. And what if I failed? I was too afraid of his rage—and the consequences—if I didn't succeed.

"Shit, shit, shit." Nix's green eyes were stark in her pale face. "He means it."

"Yeah." Del's voice shook. "We need to get those daggers."

"Now," I said.

"I wish I could just conjure a forgery," Nix said. "I really don't want to go out into the jungle tonight. Getting past the Dvarapala in the dark will suck."

Nix was a conjurer, able to create almost anything using just her magic. Massive or complex things, like airplanes or guns, were outside of her ability, but a couple of daggers wouldn't be hard.

Trouble was, they were a magical artifact, enchanted with the ability to return to whoever had thrown them. Like boomerangs. Though Nix could conjure the daggers, we couldn't enchant them.

"We need to go. We only have six hours until dawn." I grabbed my short swords from the table and stood, shoving them into the holsters strapped to my back.

A hush descended over the crowded bar.

I stiffened, but the sound of the staticky TV in the corner made me relax. They weren't interested in me. Just the news, which was probably being routed through a dozen techno-witches to get this far into the jungle.

The grave voice of the female reporter echoed through the quiet bar. "The FireSoul was apprehended outside of his apartment in Magic's Bend, Oregon. He is currently in the custody of the Order of the Magica, and his trial is scheduled for tomorrow morning. My sources report that execution is possible."

I stifled a crazed laugh. Perfect timing. Just what we needed to hear after OMB's threat. A reminder of what would happen if he turned us into the Order of the Magica. The hush that had descended over the previously rowdy crowd—the kind of hush you get at the scene of a big accident—indicated what an interesting freaking topic this was. FireSouls were the bogeymen. *I* was the bogeyman, even though I didn't use my powers. But as long as no one found out, we were safe.

My gaze darted to Del and Nix. They nodded toward the door. It was definitely time to go.

As the newscaster turned her report toward something more boring and the crowd got rowdy again, we threaded our way between the tiny tables and chairs.

I shoved the heavy wooden door open and sucked in a breath of sticky jungle air, relieved to be out of the bar. Night creatures screeched, and moonlight filtered through the trees above. The jungle would be a nice place if it weren't full of things that wanted to kill us.

"We're never escaping him, are we?" Nix said softly.

"We will." Somehow. Someday. "Let's just deal with this for now."

We found our motorcycles, which were parked in the lot

with a dozen other identical ones. They were hulking beasts with massive, all-terrain tires meant for the jungle floor. We'd done a lot of work in Southeast Asia this year, and these were our favored forms of transportation in this part of the world.

Del could transport us, but it was better if she saved her power. It wasn't infinite, though it did regenerate. But we'd learned a long time ago to save Del's power for our escape. Nothing worse than being trapped in a temple with pissed off guardians and a few tripped booby traps.

We'd scouted out the location of the temple earlier that day, so we knew where to go.

I swung my leg over Secretariat—I liked to name my vehicles —and kicked the clutch. The engine roared to life. Nix and Del followed, and we peeled out of the lot, leaving the dingy yellow light of the bar behind.

Our headlights illuminated the dirt road as we sped through the night. Huge fig trees dotted the path on either side, their twisted trunks and roots forming an eerie corridor. Elephant-ear sized leaves swayed in the wind, a dark emerald that gleamed in the light.

Jungle animals howled, and enormous lightning bugs flitted along the path. They were too big to be regular bugs, so they were most likely some kind of fairy, but I wasn't going to stop to investigate. There were dangerous creatures in the jungle at night—one of the reasons we hadn't wanted to go now—and in our world, fairies could be considered dangerous.

Especially if you called them lightning bugs.

A roar sounded in the distance, echoing through the jungle and making the leaves rustle on either side as small animals scurried for safety.

The roar came again, only closer.

Then another, and another.

"Oh shit," I muttered. This was bad.

~~~

Join my mailing list to get a free copy of *Hidden Magic.* No spam and you can leave anytime!

AUTHOR'S NOTE

Thanks for reading *Institute of Magic!* If you've read any of my previous books, you may have noticed that I have a fondness for including historical places and mythological elements. I did the same with *Institute of Magic.* Sometimes the history of these things is so interesting that I want to share more, so I like to do it in the Author's Note instead of the story itself.

Celtic myth plays a large role in Ana's series. Several side characters are from Celtic myth. Cade is actually Belatucadros, one of the Celtic war gods from Great Britain. Another character from Celtic myth is Muffin, the Cat Sìth, a type of fairy creature. In actually Celtic myth, the Cat Sìth's name isn't Muffin (that was my own addition). According to legend, he is supposed to resemble a large black cat with a white spot on his chest. The myth of the Cat Sìth was possibly inspired by the Scottish wildcat. In one British folk tale, the Cat Sìth is considered to be the king of cats. They can even steal your soul, though the Muffin in my books is more interested in stealing fish and jewels.

Muffin is hairless, however, which makes him a bit different. In the fiction wold (as opposed to the one of Celtic myth) he's the distant cousin of Magpie, a hairless cat from the Spellbound series written by Annabel Chase. I loved Magpie so much that I thought maybe my own series needed a hairless cat, and Annabel was kind enough to approve of Muffin. If you like fun paranormal cozy mysteries and you also liked Muffin, consider checking out Annabel's series and meeting Magpie.

The rest of the book draws heavily from history. Paris is indeed called the City of Lights (as are many other cities), and long ago, it was founded by the Romans as they spread across Europe. The cemetery of Père Lachaise is the largest in the city and contains a storied history. In fact, it is the most visited cemetery in the world, though of course no one can visit the supernatural section. It was established in 1804 by Napoleon and has grown astronomically since. It has been so popular that bodies are often exhumed after decomposition and their bones stored in the ossuary, where Madame Alamedra performs her ritual.

In addition to having the most famous cemetery in the world, Paris also contains the most famous sewers. They date back to 1370, though it was a much simpler system then. In the years since, it has grown massively, particularly during the 19th century. The modernization of the sewer system at this time led to a decline in epidemics, since sanitation in the city was greatly improved. Starting in the mid 19th century, it became possible to tour the sewers, which you can still do today.

Another historical aspect of *Institute of Magic* is Pompeii. The famous city was entombed in ash and pyroclastic flow from the eruption of Mount Vesuvius in 79 AD. Today, it is an amazing place. I chose to set the Pompeii scene in the baths because they were such an important part of Roman history. The baths were a common meeting place for people—both men and women— and it was common to visit the baths daily if you could afford it. In fact, it was so important that the baths were often subsidized by the government and the price was very low. One of the most interesting parts of the baths was the fact that the Romans had developed heated floors. The technology involved a hollow floor through which hot air was forced.

I think that's it for the history and mythology in *Institute of Magic*—at least the big things. I hope you enjoyed the book and will come back for more of Ana, Lachlan, Rowan, and Bree!

ACKNOWLEDGMENTS

Thank you, Ben, for everything. There would be no books without you.

Thank you to Jena O'Connor and Lindsey Loucks for your excellent editing. The book is immensely better because of you! Thank you to Eleonora for your idea to make Muffin the Cat Sith.

Thank you to Orina Kafe for the beautiful cover art. Thank you to Collette Markwardt for allowing me to borrow the Pugs of Destruction, who are real dogs named Chaos, Havoc, and Ruckus. They were all adopted from rescue agencies.

GLOSSARY

Alpha Council - There are two governments that enforce law for supernaturals—the Alpha Council and the Order of the Magica. The Alpha Council governs all shifters. They work cooperatively with the Alpha Council when necessary—for example, when capturing FireSouls.

Blood Sorcerer - A type of Magica who can create magic using blood.

Dark Magic - The kind that is meant to harm. It's not necessarily bad, but it often is.

Demons - Often employed to do evil. They live in various hells but can be released upon the earth if you know how to get to them and then get them out. If they are killed on Earth, they are sent back to their hell.

Dragon Sense - A FireSoul's ability to find treasure. It is an internal sense that pulls them toward what they seek. It is easiest to find gold, but they can find anything or anyone that is valued by someone.

Djinn - Possesses invisibility and the ability to possess others for brief periods of time.

Earthwalking Gods - Reincarnates of the ancient gods who

can walk upon the earth. They are mortal but with all the power of that god.

Enchanted Artifacts – Artifacts can be imbued with magic that lasts after the death of the person who put the magic into the artifact (unlike a spell that has not been put into an artifact —these spells disappear after the Magica's death). But magic is not stable. After a period of time—hundreds or thousands of years depending on the circumstance—the magic will degrade. Eventually, it can go bad and cause many problems.

Fire Mage – A mage who can control fire.

FireSoul - A very rare type of Magica who shares a piece of the dragon's soul. They can locate treasure and steal the gifts (powers) of other supernaturals. With practice, they can manipulate the gifts they steal, becoming the strongest of that gift. They are despised and feared. If they are caught, they are thrown in the Prison of Magical Deviants.

The Great Peace - The most powerful piece of magic ever created. It hides magic from the eyes of humans.

Magica - Any supernatural who has the power to create magic—witches, sorcerers, mages. All are governed by the Order of the Magica.

Order of the Magica - There are two governments that enforce law for supernaturals—the Alpha Council and the Order of the Magica. The Order of the Magica govern all Magica. They work cooperatively with the Alpha Council when necessary—for example, when capturing FireSouls.

Seeker - A type of supernatural who can find things. FireSouls often pass off their dragon sense as Seeker power.

Shifter - A supernatural who can turn into an animal. All are governed by the Alpha Council.

Transporter - A type of supernatural who can travel anywhere. Their power is limited and must regenerate after each use.

Undercover Protectorate - A secret organization dedicated to protecting supernaturals and solving the crimes that no one else will.

Vampire - Blood drinking supernaturals with great strength and speed who live in a separate realm.

ABOUT LINSEY

Before becoming a writer, Linsey Hall was a nautical archaeologist who studied shipwrecks from Hawaii and the Yukon to the UK and the Mediterranean. She credits fantasy and historical romances with her love of history and her career as an archaeologist. After a decade of tromping around the globe in search of old bits of stuff that people left lying about, she settled down and started penning her own romance novels. Her Dragon's Gift series draws upon her love of history and the paranormal elements that she can't help but include.

COPYRIGHT